TEQUILA SUNRISE
and other stories

BY THE SAME AUTHOR

You Are Not Alone *having the courage to defy convention* (Novel)
Story & Script (5 Short Plays)

CO-AUTHORED WITH VALERIE DUNCAN

Weeds - Poetry, Prose, Wit and Wisdom
Limericks and Trimericks
Limericks and Trimericks for Gardeners
Ziffy Bear's Book of A.B.C.
Ziffy Bear's Book of Numbers
Ziffy Bear's Book of Teddy Bear Poems

ANTHOLOGIES

Wednesday's Words - Christchurch Writer's Group
Best of Cafe Lit 10 - Chapeltown Books
COVID 19: An Extraordinary Time - Chapeltown Books

TEQUILA SUNRISE
and other stories

A Collection of short stories

Greg Duncan

Kenebec Media

www.kenebec.com/books

First published in Great Britain by Kenebec Media 2022

ISBN (Paperback): 9798428514292
ISBN (Hardback): 9798428515411

INTRODUCTION

This collection of short stories embraces a variety of styles including tales with unexpected twist endings and romantic stories along with a smattering of thought provoking items. In length they vary from single page flash stories to multi-part short sagas.

Most of these items were read to the members of the Christchurch Writers Group meeting in Christchurch, Dorset. Their comments have been appreciated and have often lead to subtle changes. A few of the pieces have been previously published in the Group's Anthology Collection – *Wednesday's Words*.

The author would particularly like to thank Caz Nolder, Frances Duncan and Janet Gogerty for reading and commenting on the original draft of this book.

THE STORIES

TEQUILA SUNRISE

"I liked your presentation. Can I ask you some questions over coffee?"

"Glad you liked it, but no thanks – I already have plans."

Although Lara enjoyed giving presentations, it was the book signing afterwards she dreaded. Too often the title of her self-help book, *'Take Control of Your Life',* was misinterpreted by men in the audience as an opportunity to practice their chat-up lines. Many saw the week-end conferences as a time for a secret dalliance and fancied their chances with the speaker. But that was not Lara's way.

Their smarmy lines reminded Lara only too vividly of her failed relationship with Matt. Their interests were similar but not overlapping – his was business and photography – hers was psychology and art. To their friends they appeared to be well suited but with time underlying differences and tensions emerged. She thought there was commitment – he didn't. She thought there was honesty – he had no qualms about lying. The final straw came when she discovered his photography sessions included more than just taking pictures of the nude models.

The split was nasty and Lara felt deeply hurt and betrayed. But instead of wallowing in self-pity, she used her experience and training to advantage. Her book on taking control of your own life became a best seller and soon she was a sought after speaker at business conferences. However, with respect to men and relationships, the words *'never again'* were always on her mind.

Although she had enjoyed her intimacy with Matt, Lara knew that for her, honesty and emotional compatibility were much more important and critical. She certainly was not interested in becoming someone's secret throw away fling.

So now the stock answer to these unwanted invitations was, "Glad you liked it, but no thanks – I already have plans." If she was not needed later in a conference, Lara's plans would be to head home rather than stay over. It was on one such return trip home that she was involved in a car accident.

At a downtown intersection, the light was red so she had stopped. The shiny black BMW behind her had also stopped. Unfortunately the driver of the van behind that car was looking at his phone and ploughed into the car so hard it had shunted forward and hit Lara's car.

Before Lara could even undo her seat belt, the BMW driver was at her window. "Are you alright? Are you hurt? There was nothing I could do – the van behind hit me and pushed me into your car."

"Thanks for asking but I'm OK. I saw what was happening in my mirror and braced myself. But I guess we need to exchange details for the insurance. I'm Lara Petro. I'll get you one of my cards." Lara reached in her bag and then stepped out of the car to look at the damage.

"I'm Kelvin March and here's my card."

When Lara looked at the BMW she saw there was someone in the passenger seat. "Is your companion OK? She does not appear to have moved?"

Kelvin reassured her, "Alexie's fine. A bit shaken but otherwise just annoyed. We were going out for dinner and she'd spent a long time getting ready. She might need a moment or two on her own, if you know what I mean."

As they surveyed the two cars a policeman came over. He had been parked on the other side of the road, had seen the full incident and confirmed that the van driver was fully at fault. Unfortunately, he also expressed the opinion that with respect to the two cars, neither vehicle was now in a safe state to continue. They would both need to be towed away. For safety reasons, he advised them not to stay in the cars and that they should perhaps wait in the coffee shop across the road.

Alexie did not consider a latte and a chocolate muffin a suitable alternative to the fancy dinner she'd been looking forward to. She remained in a huff while Lara and Kelvin talked freely. Their friendliness towards each other only increased Alexie's bad mood and Kelvin was not looking forward to the aftermath of this evening.

Kelvin's position as a project manager with a large consultancy firm meant he often worked at the client's offices. It was at one such job he had met Alexie. She was gorgeous, single and had made a strong play for Kelvin's attention. Since he was also single, he did not object and soon they became an item. After only two months, she effectively moved into his apartment and took over his life.

However, he soon discovered that she could display amazing mood swings and she appeared to be much more interested in being seen with him than being with him. When his job took him away to various events to which she was not invited, she even suggested he should change job. An unlikely option.

As part of his training to become a senior project manager, Kelvin was sent on a two day workshop on team development. To his surprise, one of the guest speakers on the opening evening was Lara. After the accident, he had bought her first book and this evening he was so enthralled by her presentation he decided to purchase her second book.

While waiting in the queue to have her sign it, he heard her stock refusal to invitations, "Glad you liked it, but no thanks – I already have plans."

He needed a different approach. "Fancy bumping into you again – if I recall correctly, it's a cappuccino with two sugars?"

Lara looked up, recognized Kelvin and with a smile changed her reply, "A much nicer way to meet – no damage this time. Yes please Kelvin – you're right – it's two sugars. But just wait – I won't be long here."

When they sat down with their drinks Kelvin remarked, "You weren't down as one of the speakers – I would have noticed. I was impressed by your other book."

"The speaker was taken ill and they asked if I could step in at the last minute. I didn't have time to check the attendees or I would have contacted you. Is Alice here with you?"

"Alexie, actually. No she doesn't come to these events."

"You're still together though?"

"Yes. She wants me to change my job and I'm not keen. But otherwise we're fine. And how about you?"

"Just the same – quite happily on my own. It'll take a special man to get my attention and from what I see, all the good ones are taken and the others can't be trusted."

Kelvin smiled, "I noticed that sentiment in your other book where you state – 'without honesty and trust – a relationship is just a convenience'. Many in my line of business appear, unfortunately, to choose the dishonest convenience option. Talking of business, how is the art side working out for you?"

"Well thanks. Not only am I selling some but I'm now teaching art at adult education classes."

"That's great – are you enjoying it?"

The conversation continued to flow easily and Lara wished Kelvin was not still with Alexie. But he was taken and therefore out of bounds.

As eleven o'clock approached Kelvin stood up, "I've got some work to do for tomorrow. Are you running the workshop?"

"Yes, so you better be a good boy."

"I'll try. See you tomorrow then." And Kelvin went upstairs alone.

Lara found herself being strongly attracted to him. Apart from his good looks, she felt at ease with him. He had not tried to make a pass or in any sense hit on her. She realized that *'never again'* might be too strong but only if she could find an available person she could trust.

The concept of trust became a major issue for Kelvin soon after he returned home from the workshop. Alexie saw the book he bought at the workshop and confronted him. "What's the meaning of this? When were you going to tell me about your fancy lady? This book's signed by the author *'To Kelvin, With memories, Lara'*. I thought you could be trusted and yet this is what you are up to when you're away? I just don't believe what a fool I've been."

"Alexie – look at the author – she is the lady we bumped into – that's what she meant by 'memories' – memories of the crash. She was one of the main speakers and I bought her book. That's all."

"That's all you're going to tell me, is what you mean. You've probably kept her business card she gave you at the accident. How often have you been meeting her? I just can't believe this. And I trusted you but not now – how can I when you are willing to tell me such lies."

"Alexie – phone her up and ask her. Nothing has ever happened."

"Yeh like I'm going to ask her *'did you sleep with my man?'* No she'll just lie to me as well – the conniving bitch. And you fell for it."

Kelvin thought about the line in Lara's other book – the line about trust, honesty and relationships.

"If you think I'm lying to you, which I'm not, why are you still here? If your opinion of me is that low, what kind of a relationship is this? I just don't —"

Alexie stopped him mid-sentence. "Don't worry Kelvin. I'll be gone within the hour. There is no way I'm living with a liar like you. You're such a — I don't have words to describe my feelings. Just shut-up and let me pack."

Kelvin sat down and said nothing more. In his mind he knew Lara was right. If there is no trust, there is no relationship and he was not going to try and stop Alexie. He decided not to ask her about the five day Mediterranean cruise he and Alexie had booked as she would just tell him to take his *'fancy woman'*.

The apartment felt quiet after she left and he looked up the cruise details. They had been due to sail in three weeks and the contract was clear – no refund within 28 days. Since he had already arranged holiday time, he decided he might as well go, even on his own and just enjoy the break.

Although he did think about Lara, he could hardly ask her to go on a cruise with him when they hadn't even been on a proper date. He admitted to himself that he was attracted to her but equally he didn't want to hear her brush off line, *'No thanks – I already have plans'*.

So three weeks later, on the day when the cruise liner set sail and he stood alone at the upper deck cocktail bar, Kelvin was at ease with himself. He saw the cruise as a time to plan what he really wanted out of life. But then a soft whisper broke his peace and quiet.

"Ordering just one drink? Not two?"

Kelvin recognized the voice and swung around, "Lara? What are you doing here?"

"I'm part of the ship's entertainment crew. I'll be teaching art classes in the evening. So where's Alexie?"

"Short story – she's gone. Long story – she read the inscription you wrote in the book and accused me of lying and cheating. She didn't believe anything I said when I told her nothing had happened."

"Oh I am sorry – I didn't mean anything to come between you two. Oh damn – you must be really angry with me. I'll go."

"No please don't. I thought about your words on trust and relationships – no trust – no relationship. You were so right."

"When Alexie left, you should've called me – if you still have my card."

"I do have it – and I wanted to call you – yes – certainly. But I couldn't presume that you would particularly want to see me."

At his words Lara felt a warm tingle scurry down her spine. A tingle that told her to stop being so obstinately stupid. She listened to that tingle, leant forward and planted a soft kiss on Kelvin's lips. They were warm and receptive.

"If you feel like ordering two drinks, mine's a Tequila Sunrise."

THE STORY MAKER

When Chris brought the adult education creative writing class to order with his customary, "Good evening writers," the group responded back with their usual, "Good evening."

Chris then set the topic for the session. "Tonight I want to ask you – how short can a story be? What is the fewest number of words you need to make a story?"

Nora responded with, "Perhaps, a hundred and fifty words?"

Darren countered that. "No, no. I've seen flash fiction competitions for one hundred words."

Chris nodded. "Any reduction on one hundred words?"

Marg suggested, "Maybe fifty words but that's probably too short."

There were some questioning looks when Chris stated, "Six words. That's all."

He continued. "Apparently at a dinner with fellow writers, Ernest Hemingway bet his friends he could write a story in just six words. They called his bluff and he then wrote just six words on a napkin and won the bet."

Marg questioned this. "Just six words? Ok, what are they?"

Chris wrote them on the board. "For sale; baby shoes; never worn."

Marg immediately responded. "That's so sad."

Nora agreed with a slight sniffle. "That brings tears to my eyes."

There ensued a general discussion on how powerful the story was – how it invoked a major sense of loss. Someone raised the point, "It leaves us wondering how the baby died." Others commented on how superbly the author conveyed his meaning with so few words. There was general agreement that Hemingway's six words were all that was needed to convey everything he wanted us to feel.

When Kevin finally spoke, his comment was received with derision from his fellow class mates when he said, "That's not a story – it's merely a prompt. There is no story there."

Nora was almost disgusted. "How can you call yourself a writer when you have no sense of empathy? That's a complete tragic story."

After a few similar derisory remarks, Chris, the tutor, asked Kevin to explain.

"I said it was a prompt and not a story because you have no idea at all what the author wanted you to feel. You all see it as tragic, sad, even almost morbid but you have no idea if that is what the author was trying to convey."

Even Darren disagreed. "Come on Kevin, look at it again. Look at the words – read them again. It's a complete tragic story in just 6 words. We know exactly what Hemingway meant and the rest of us understand it. Sorry Kev, but you're way out on this."

At this point Chris interjected. "I was hoping someone would raise the point Kevin has made. You may want to disagree but perhaps he's right. Is it a complete story or is it just a prompt from which the rest of you have become authors of your own fiction based on those words?"

Most of the class muttered in disagreement but Chris continued. "It's an interesting conundrum – the shorter the story, the more the reader becomes a major part of the story-making process. They become almost authors of a story they think the writer had in mind, based purely on a prompt. In one of Jane Austin's novels, there is little for you to fill in. She tells you exactly what she wants you to feel. Here Hemingway, assuming it was him, has given you a prompt and you have created a story. Think about it, each of your stories will be slightly different but apart from Kevin here, you all seem to be thinking along the same tragic line."

Marg could not hold back. "No way. That's not a prompt – it's a full story. *'For sale; baby shoes; never worn'*. Just 'cause Kevin can't understand the underlying sadness doesn't make it a prompt. It's a complete sad story."

Chris looked at the class. "You're not alone in seeing the sadness. It's interesting to note that with respect to these six words, the author, Arthur C Clarke, wrote *'I still can't think of it without crying'*. So – with the exception of Kevin, are we in agreement that these six words are indeed a complete sad story and not just a prompt and that we only needed to see those six words to know exactly what the author wanted us to feel?"

There was general agreement.

Chris smiled and turned the page in his notes. "I've got something to read to you – just one hundred and fifty words and when I finish I'll ask you again. Are these six words a story or just a prompt? Based only on those six words, do we really have any idea what Hemingway wanted us to feel?" At that point Chris read the following.

> "Parcel for Mrs McOwen   from Little Shoes."
> "Parcel from Little Shoes for Mrs McOwen   ."
> They just kept coming. Different delivery companies but the contents were always the same. Little shoes for Abigail's Christening. It seemed as if every aunt and uncle had gone on-line with the same great idea. A pair of pink booties!
> However, Abigail was quite normal. She only had two feet and didn't need 12 pairs, lovely though they were.
> "Malcolm. Can't any of our relations think of something else. A Christening spoon would have been nice."
> "Are they all the same?"

"Yes. Identical."

"We could exchange eleven of them and get a spoon. Everybody would think Abigail was wearing the pair they gave her."

"No, Malcolm, we don't have receipts so we can't return them."

"Ok, let's sell them. Classified ads?"

She nodded in agreement and they drafted their ad.

"For sale; baby shoes; never worn."

When Chris finished, there was silence in the class. He asked once more. "The same six words – sad or happy? — On their own, as they were when Hemingway wrote them, there is no context. So, are those six words a full story or just a prompt into YOUR subconscious? What does your response say about you the reader? Basically, who is the story maker here – Hemingway or you?"

After a few moments Marg asked the tutor a simple question. "Do all stories act as prompts for our imagination?"

Chris answered. "Good question — and I'll leave you to answer it."

THE INTERVIEW

When Mr Jones asked downstairs, he had been told to take the lift to the third floor, turn right and go through the double doors. He pushed the doors aside with an air of superiority only to find that he was now in a short hallway with two empty chairs. At the end of the hall was another door with a sign *'Wait here until you are called'*.

He sat down trying not to crumple his shiny blue suit. After a short while his impatience took hold and he began to fidget and twiddle his thumbs.

The double doors swung open again. A woman in a dark coloured business suit enquired rather timidly. "Is this Oberlong Industries?"

"Yeh. Hope so. Damn well better be."

The new arrival sat on the other chair and asked another question. "Are you here for the job interview as well?"

"Yep, 4:30 appointment."

"That's odd – same as me. What's the time now?"

Mr Jones looked at his watch with a flourish to make sure she saw his gold bling.

"It's already gone 4:30 – they're late."

"Wow, that's a nice watch – Rolex?"

"Yeh, well – maybe – maybe not – I got it in Hong Kong so – you know what I mean. But it looks good. Eh?"

"Yeh – I was told that appearances are everything."

"You're right there. Number one rule – first impression is critical."

There ensued a period of silence. Then she spoke again. "I don't know about you, but I'm nervous, This is my first interview."

"First interview? Do they do a second interview here? I thought they said they would be offering the job today."

"No no – MY first interview. I've never done a job interview like this before and really don't know how to handle it. And as for sales – that's not my game at all – I would hate it."

"Did you say you hate sales?"

"Yeh – no way – that's not me."

Mr Jones looked at her with a sneer. "So why are you applying for this job, dear? As a sales manager?"

"I know – it sounds dumb but I thought I need to learn – I need to gain interview experience and why blow my chances on a job I might actually want. So here I am – but sales? Absolutely NO."

"And you've never had a job interview? Never?"

"No never – not like this. I have read some books about it – you know *'dress well, be on time, be honest'* etc."

"Yeh – well take it from me, lady, some of that's real stupid. Le'me tell you. The number one rule – honesty in an interview is for losers."

"Honesty is for losers? Surely not. Surely you … really? But what do you mean?"

"Ok – your CV – have you been honest or made it sound better than the truth?"

"Well honest of course."

"No no, you're being stupid. Exaggerate everything. That's the number one rule. If you got bad grades, boost them up – they never check. If you've had a lousy job, invent some important sounding thing you had to do – again – they never check. Number one rule – make yourself sound bigger and better than you are."

"Interesting – very interesting. I think I see where you're going."

There was another period of silence after which she again started a conversation. "You've done this before haven't you?"

"Yeh – it's how you move up. Apply for a job – work at it for a while – apply for another – exaggerate what you did – get the next job, and it goes on – that's the number one rule, love."

"Always in sales? Have you done this all the time in sales?"

Our man in the shiny blue suit was now in his element. "Yeh – I'm a top salesman – George Jones at your service ma'am. That's me and I'm great at it." He leaned towards her and smiled. "And it means I earn big bonuses."

"Oh. So why are YOU here?"

"In the last place, one of the contracts went a bit south if you know what I mean. You might say the customer perhaps got slightly less than they were expecting?"

"You mean you lied?"

"Come on – you can't be that naive. Number one rule in sales – tell the customer what they want to hear – not what you can provide. That would be stupid."

"If that's right – it's certainly not for me. I couldn't do that."

"Hey – since you're not really wanting this job, le'me tell you. Sales is all about conning the customer. Over state what the product can do. Get them excited – it doesn't matter – I'm never the one who has to provide the product – that's production's job – not mine. That's the number one rule in sales – over sell the product and over sell yourself."

"Yeh?"

"The bigger the lie – the bigger the contract – the bigger the bonus and the easier it is to get the next job. Keep on moving – that's the number one rule."

"You make it sound so easy but I just don't think I could do that. Trying to persuade people to do things they wouldn't otherwise do? No – that's not me – not sales."

Silence descended again. George began to have a smug smile as he realized that the job would be his – he could see this lady was no threat.

However, after a while curiosity won and George asked a question. "Ok. If you're not in sales, what is it you do then?"

"I'm more of a scientist."

"What – experiments an' that kin' a stuff?"

"Yeh we design experiments and see if they work. See if the results are what we expect."

"And if they aren't – d'you fudge the results? I mean, are you always honest? Or d'you do a bit of exaggerating – you know – kind'a like us sales boys?"

"Well, sometimes we need to hide what we are doing during the experiments."

"Hide your experiments, eh? Dangerous chemicals and all that stuff. So, le'me understand. When the men have finished doing an experiment you come in and clean the place up, eh? Do the guys ever let you do any of the actual experiments?"

"Actually we work with people not chemicals."

"Experiments on people? That sounds weird. Gi'me an example."

"Actually that's quite easy to give you an example."

"Easy? How?"

"Well let me put it this way. You've been the experiment and I think we'll stop this chat now and I'll just say thank you Mr Jones for your time. I think you have told us here at Oberlong, all we need to know about you."

George sat up a bit straighter. "What do you mean – I've been the experiment? What are you saying?"

"Well let me put it another way. Oberlong Industries has been trying out a new interviewing technique in which we aim to assess an applicant's adaptability, personality and above all their honesty in an unexpected setting – right here – in the hall – right now. That's why there are only two chairs."

George's face took on a menacing look. "I don't think I fully understand."

"OK – I'll be more explicit. Our discussion has been your interview for the job. Given the things you've said about yourself and your attitude towards honesty and the companies you've worked for, I think you'll understand when I say there is no way I will be recommending you for the job. Sorry, but Oberlong Industries will not be offering you the sales manager's job. Thank you Mr Jones for coming along but the answer is no. Can you find your own way back?"

"What? You cannot be serious. You were interviewing me all this time? Typical damn deceiving two-faced woman. So that's how Oberlong operates – glad I found out in time. What a shower! I'm leaving right now and don't bother to write – I wouldn't work for Oberlong – not now – not never."

As our blue suited salesman barged out through the double doors he was still expressing his displeasure. "Underhanded dirty tricks – unbelievable! I'm getting out of here right now while I can. Goodbye!"

The double doors swung closed and there was silence again.

The lady reached in her bag for a mirror and checked her hair and makeup.

After a pause, the other door opened and Gwen entered carrying an official looking clipboard. She looked perplexed. "Have you seen a gentleman here, a Mr Jones?"

"There was somebody here – a George Jones? He seemed really annoyed – kept looking at his watch and said something about never wanting to work for Oberlong anyway and stomped out."

"Oh pity – he looked quite promising. And you are?"

"Catherine Malloway. I've a 5 o'clock appointment. I'm applying for the sales manager's job."

Gwen looked at her clipboard. "Ah yes. I see you're early but come on in."

Author's Note

Although originally written as a story, it has been converted into a one act short play and included in the collection of short plays *'Story & Script Vol 1'*.

MURDER IS THE PROBLEM

One solitary bulb hung on a spindly wire from the ceiling. The dim light it gave was almost overpowered by the smog of cigarette smoke. Five men sat around the table waiting for the boss. When Bruce opened the door and stood with arms crossed over his chest, they knew they had got it wrong. With a glower that could make black storm clouds look friendly he snarled at them, "Murder is not what I suggested."

A deathly silence ensued.

Finally Ronnie spoke up. "You wanted him removed – dat's what you said. So dat's what we done."

"Removed – yes – but not murdered. I never suggested murder. I'm away for two days and this is what happens. What the blazes got into you? All of you."

"You wanted him out of the scene and murder sure does dat – He ain't comin' back – he can't say nothin' – dead men don't tell no tales – der's no problem."

Bruce made his incensed feelings known loudly. "No problem? No Problem? Have you guys not got any idea of the problems this creates?"

Another electrifying silence engulfed the men.

Little Bob, the one with 'mother' tattooed on his upper arm, spoke up in a questioning stuttering tone. "I – I don't see no problem – wha – wha – what d'you mean problem? He's out of it."

Incredulity spread across Bruce's face. Then with his arms gesticulating wildly he explained what he meant. "Murder means police. Police means an investigation. An investigation upsets the plans. There's no way we can ignore a murder investigation – it alters everything. What a mess you've made."

Charlie offered a solution. "Should we make it look like suicide? Write some suicide note?"

In exasperation Bruce screamed at him. "Suicide? Are you out of your mind?"

"Why not – many people like him kill 'emselves."

"Yeh – but not by stabbing themselves in the back, you idiot. A knife in the front – maybe. A knife in the back – no way – everybody knows that can only be murder – plain an' simple. Why a knife in the back? Why murder?"

Jimmy tried to put forth a justification for murder. "Why murder? Well, no one liked him – look at the things he did – think of Roger and how he treated him. He'll have to remain in hospital for months. And then there was that issue with Buster — you won't see him saying he's upset with murder. In fact, here's an idea – perhaps with a bit of *help*, the investigation could, er, could show that Buster did it?"

Bruce clenched his fists and pounded the table. "I know all that. In some ways I agree but I never suggested murder. None of our plans included murder! All I said was we need to get rid of him. Stop trying to sugar coat your damn mistakes."

With despair written across his face Bruce turned his attention to Roy and Roy knew that look and knew what was coming. "Roy, you need to fix this and fix it NOW."

"OK Bruce. You're the boss. We'll change it – no murder. We can do it again. How about a fatal car accident?"

Bruce nodded his agreement and the TV production team shuffled out leaving Roy and Jimmy to rewrite the script ready for the actors in the morning, changing death by murder to death by a car accident.

Problem solved.

I wrote this piece with intentional misdirection to imply a strong element of criminality. To maintain the allusion, I decided all eight names mentioned should have an inherent criminal association. As a consequence, although they were not in anyway involved in murder, I chose all the names for this story from the list of people convicted of the *'Great Train Robbery'* of August 1963 when a gang of fifteen people stopped and robbed a Royal Mail Train carrying used money on its way to be destroyed. Since Bruce Reynolds was regarded as having been the leader behind the robbery, I used the name Bruce as the producer of the TV show mentioned in this story.

GRANDPA RALPH

When his widowed mother passed away, Elliot had the unenviable task of clearing out her house. Although inherently a sad activity, he soon discovered that she had been more of a hoarder than he had realized. In the attic he found boxes containing special items, old letters, postcards and other memorabilia.

One box was of particular interest. With the enticing label, *Family Pics,* it was a shoe box of old photographs. Elliot had often been told about his grandfather Ralph and hoped there might be a picture of this man in the box. Apparently Ralph had been a larger than life person, the soul of a party, a generous man who Elliot would have loved to have met.

Physically Elliot had taken after his father's side so there was unlikely to be any facial resemblance but at least there was a chance this box might contain an image of the man, enabling Elliot to see what Ralph looked like.

Elliot took the old box down from the attic, opened it on the kitchen table and began pulling out the photographs one at a time. First there was an image of a lady in a starched dress. He turned it over and read *Aunt Laura*. He'd heard of this aunt and here was a picture of her. Another photograph was of a couple at one of those pier photograph spots. He turned it over – *Miles and Melissa*. Not a couple he knew.

There were more images depicting people he'd heard of. Elliot was becoming quite enthralled and excited as each picture was documented precisely with names on the back.

One group were identified as *James, Bill and Ethel*. His mother had often spoken of Aunt Ethel. He continued extracting pictures, looking closely at them and turning them over to read the names – some of which he knew – others he assumed were the names of friends.

At the bottom of the box was an old envelope with an inscription – *Ralph's Photos*. Had his mother been given these when Ralph passed away? Eagerly Elliot carefully pulled back the envelope's flap and pulled out just three photographs. The first was of a Victorian styled lady sitting primly on a chair in front of a back drop of roses. The back had one word – *Felicity*. Felicity? Was that one of Grandpa Ralph's girlfriends? There was no one now to ask.

The next image was of a young lad – *Dermott* was written on the back. Dermott? Elliot recognized the name – some distant great uncle he was if Elliot remembered rightly.

And finally there was a picture of four lads standing together obviously enjoying themselves. One of these must be Grandpa Ralph. Elliot studied all four closely as he tried to determine which would turn out to be his ancestor.

Having decided which was most likely Ralph, Elliot looked on the back to see if he was right. And there he read words which had been written many decades before.

'Me and the others last Thursday'.

After laughing at the cryptic message, Elliot spoke to himself, "Thanks Ralph – that's not a lot of help."

TWO OF THEM

They sat patiently on the wall, eyeing the people passing by. The two of them often sat there in the sun as if they owned the place. Theirs had been a very rough and traumatic upbringing. They had not known their father and then just as they were beginning to understand the world, their mother disappeared. She just left one day and never came back.

For this pair, there was no social safety net – no relations to shoulder the burden of helping them. They had to learn to fend for themselves and learn fast. Being two of them, they helped each other and soon found how to survive in this challenging world.

Their life revolved around begging for food but often people would either turn away or try to frighten them. Nobody really seemed to care. Some sanctimonious parents thought it was quaint or educational to let their children feed them but the pair did not adopt any form of false pride – survival dictated they accept whatever they were given.

It appeared as if over time they developed a keen sense of opportunity. Although it was not possible to make out what they were saying to each other, you could see the pair would look at each passing person and assess if they could be a target and a possible source of food. One could almost hear them say, "Look at that couple, the one with the small child. Let's wait to see if they have anything of interest." And if the people had food then off the pair would go.

With no warning they would swoop down, grab the fish and chips in their beaks, flick their wings with force and fly out to sea to consume their ill gotten gains leaving their victims cursing at the local gulls.

Author's Note

Unfortunately, the underlying tale comes from personal experience and the gulls who attacked the sausage and chips I was carrying were able to splatter ketchup all over my shirt.

THE CAMERA

Stella placed the suitcase on her bed. The clothes for the trip were already laid out in neat piles. Warm sweaters, extra gloves, many pairs of thick socks, a furry hat. She had studied the suggested list of clothing and was taking no chances. Iceland in early spring could still be very cold.

After the divorce, Stella had resumed her fascination with photography. Free now to choose what she wanted to do, Stella had joined a camera club. It was filled with friendly people who were interested in taking pictures and not in starting relationships. That suited Stella perfectly as she wanted time on her own to recover from her abusive controlling ex. She was enjoying being single and had no plans to change that.

It was Carly at the camera club who had encouraged her to go on this photographic adventure. "Come on Stella. Have you ever seen a real glacier?"

"No. But I've never gone on such a trip on my own. I'm not sure."

"You wouldn't be on your own. Tristen and I will be going and so will Donna. There'll also be some people from other clubs. Twelve of us in total. It could be just what you need. It's time for you to build new memories and forget the past."

It was Carly's last line that persuaded her. And so there she was – zipping up her suitcase and waiting for the taxi to take her to the airport shuttle bus.

She looked again at the list of people who would be travelling with her. Some she knew but others she'd never heard of. Why didn't the organizer show their full names? Who was M Thompson? And was B Kelly a man or a woman? She told herself this was part of the adventure – meeting new people who shared a common interest.

In another part of town, Ben Kelly was packing and repacking his camera bag. From bitter experience he had learned *take everything you can – something will always go wrong.* Two cameras, multiple lenses, extra batteries, battery chargers. He was much more concerned about his camera gear than his clothing. He'd been on cold trips before and packing the suitcase was almost instinctive. It was also so much easier since Patricia had moved out. He didn't need to put her excess clothing in his suitcase. When he thought about it, he really didn't miss her – their attraction had been mainly physical and they had very little in common.

He was ready when his taxi called.

Stella hated being late so she arrived at the airport well ahead of time. Sitting in a coffee shop with a slowly cooling latte she was enjoying studying all the bustle. There were mothers dragging tired kids; there were groups of men trying to be more nonchalant than their peers; there were older couples pulling exceedingly large suitcases – *were they taking all their possessions on holiday?* And then there were the anxious ones jumping up to look at the departure board every minute. And others slouched in their chairs as if this was the first time they had ever sat down.

As the agreed meeting time approached, she gathered up her cases and trundled towards the main clock beside the bookshop. There were some people there but no one she knew. Her heart sank – *what am I doing?* At that point Carly and Tristen came up behind her, "I see you've made it in good time Stella. Have you met the others?"

Carly rattled off a string of names that Stella felt sure she would forget. Apparently they were missing two people but at that point Derrick spoke up. "Oh there they are."

Stella looked over to see a gorgeous dark haired man about her age with a smile to curl your toes. However, she also noticed that his arm was around the shoulders of an attractive lady who was smiling at him. Were one of these the B Kelly in the list?

She wondered what her face had revealed when the couple walked straight up to her, "Hi. I'm Ben Kelly and this is Maureen Thompson. I don't recall seeing you before on one of these trips. We're with the Shutterbug Club."

His handshake sent a tingle up her arm. Not a bad tingle – just not one she was expecting. Trying to regain her composure and not stutter, Stella replied, "No, this is my first trip with the Shadow Club. It's all kind of new to me but I'm looking forward to it."

Stella's thoughts were running wild and she reminded herself this was a photographic trip and anyway Ben was here with Maureen – *so grow up girl and mingle with the others. You're here to take pictures – not ogle men.*

The flight to Iceland was uneventful. Apart from the joy of eating rather stale sandwiches, the most exciting aspect was trying to decide between coffee and tea – neither of which looked enticing. Although they were travelling as a group, the seat allocation process had not taken that into account. As a consequence, Stella found herself sitting between a taciturn girl who pretended she could not speak English and a rather snooty man who spent his time reading the *Financial Times*.

Fortunately it was not a long flight and before she became completely bored, the plane landed. The customs and immigration officers were efficient and courteous which meant soon she was reunited with her luggage and her companions.

The trip organizer had arranged three self drive jeeps. There was no particular allocation so Stella joined Carly, Tristen and Donna in the second jeep. Given all the suitcases and equipment people had brought she saw why they needed six seater vehicles. The back row was soon covered with bags, tripods, overcoats and hats.

After a quick tour of Reykjavik to view the modern cathedral, the convoy drove for three hours to the first hotel, stopping along the way to take pictures. Stella particularly liked the picture she took of the little red roofed church sitting on a hill overlooking Vik, a fishing village. She decided she would print it and use it as her next year's Christmas card.

By the time they reached the hotel Stella was already pleased she had agreed to go on this trip. They would be staying in this hotel for three days so rooms were assigned and everything unpacked before the evening meal. Since most of the group had met on previous trips, the meal and subsequent coffee time were lively. Stella's concerns about not knowing people were ill founded. Even though she only knew a few of them, they took the effort to include her in their conversations and she rapidly felt welcomed and involved. They would be getting up early to catch the sunrise so everyone went off to bed by nine o'clock.

The following day after a hearty breakfast, they all clambered into the jeeps before first light and drove to the selected spot by the sea. Without hesitation most of the group wandered off to find their own 'perfect spot' and set up their tripods and cameras. Stella felt a bit at a loss and it must have shown. Carly noticed. "Is this the first time you've done early morning landscape photography?"

"I hate to admit it but yes. I'm not sure what settings I need."

"I see you've got the same type of camera as Tristen. He'll help you." And with that she called him over. Tristen enjoyed teaching photography and soon Stella was clicking away with a smile on her face. By the end of the day, she was photographing the stunning scenery like an old pro.

However, half way through the following day, her smile turned to a yelp of frustration. "Does anyone know what Error 72 means?"

The closest person was Ben who stopped what he was doing and walked over, "Did you say Error 72?"

"Yes. The camera seems to have stopped and no matter what I do it keeps showing that error."

"I've seen it before. Sorry to say but Error 72 can only be fixed at a repair shop. Have you got another camera with you?"

"No. I could only afford the one. How could this happen? And we have another 5 days to go. I guess I'll just have to sit and watch. Oh damn! And I was so enjoying this!"

Ben did not need to see the tears welling in her eyes to know she was deeply upset. He'd had a similar experience himself which was why he always travelled with two cameras.

"No you can't stop. Not here with this beautiful scenery. Here, you can borrow one of my cameras."

"What? Thanks but I couldn't do that – you need both of them."

"Stella. I only have one tripod so I only need one camera at a time. Please. I mean it. It's not the same make as yours so you'll need to use some of my lenses but I'm sure we can work something out if we stay close together."

Stella was not sure what made her more excited – having someone lend her a camera or working close to the disarmingly attractive Ben. He had an easy going manner as he taught her how to use the new camera and didn't seem to mind the time he was spending with her. Neither did she. There was no tension and they worked well together with much jovial banter.

Two days later Stella had a quiet word with Carly after dinner. "I feel awful about Ben. He's being so helpful."

"And how's that a problem? Come on – he's one of the nicest guys you'll ever meet. And admit it – he's not bad looking."

"Yes I know and that's part of the problem. He's spending so much time with me and Maureen is showing no jealousy at all."

Carly couldn't help laughing, "Did you say Maureen's not being jealous?"

"No. In fact she's been annoyingly understanding."

"Why did you think she would be jealous?"

"Well you saw them at the airport arm in arm smiling at each other. Oh this trip is becoming awkward. And stop laughing – I'm being serious."

Carly continued to chuckle, "Stella dear. There's a very good reason why Maureen isn't jealous. Ben and Maureen are brother and sister. She told me she hadn't seen Ben so happy in ages."

All Stella could manage was, "Oh — That changes things a bit!"

Carly leant forward, "I've another little secret for you that might change things even more."

"You've already said a lot. What more can you add?"

"Earlier today Ben asked me *'Is Stella, that stunning redhead, attached to anyone?'* I told him no. Put simply – go for it girl. He's single. You could even make me jealous."

Stella found sleep that night rather difficult. Dreams of Ben kept floating through her mind. Her time with her ex had been so unpleasant she was not sure she could remember how to flirt. But then she wasn't dreaming of just a flirt. Perhaps a kiss? Perhaps? No. She kept telling herself she didn't want another relationship. But secretly she knew this wasn't true.

The following morning everyone was at the coast photographing the waves crashing over the black sands. Ben suggested to Stella she use one of his telephoto lenses to capture the spray against the far rocks.

"Which rocks do you mean?"

She meant it as a serious question and was not prepared for Ben's response. He stood behind her putting his arm gently on her shoulder with his outstretched hand pointing to a series of rocks along the coast. She leant back against his chest, felt her heart rate increase and turned her head towards him, "Carly told me something about you yesterday."

Ben swung her around so that they were standing leaning against each other. "Really? And what might that be?"

Stella recalled Carly's words and decided *don't tell him — show him*. So she put her arms around his neck and pulled his face towards her. In the cold Icelandic air, the kiss felt soft and warm and seemed to last for ever. She felt his arms wrap around her which was good as her legs were turning to jelly. When they finally stopped and gazed at each other Ben was the first to speak.

"Carly has a way with words, doesn't she?"

And then with a smile capable of melting an iceberg, "Do you think I should join your camera club?"

Stella replied with a rather husky whisper. "It wasn't the camera club I was thinking you should join."

The twinkle in his eyes said more than his words. "And what might you mean by that?"

In reply, Stella closed her eyes, wriggled in his arms and started an even more passionate embrace. Her resolve against entering a new relationship was disappearing fast.

I was always told when travelling on a photographic excursion, it is advisable to take two cameras. I discovered the appropriateness of this advice when on a trip to Iceland the shutter in one of my cameras stopped working. Fortunately I had a second one with me. But that is the only similarity between my experience and the story.

DEFIANCE

"I can't believe you did it." —— Her trembling voice echoed around their tiny apartment.

They had both talked about doing such a dangerous act. Removing the yellow jude star from his jacket could lead to being arrested or even shot. She was too afraid to do the same. She had lost faith in humanity. Her daily trudge across the cobbled plaza was always under the scrutiny of the local Gestapo. Gone was the enjoyment of life replaced now with the diktats of survival.

"Kurt, please sew it back on – do it now – one person alone can not defeat the system. Not now. You've heard the news from Warsaw."

"But we need to stand up for freedom."

"The way you're going, you won't be standing at all – you will be lying. Lying dead and where will that leave me. You promised not to leave me – so please, let me find some thread. I'll sew it back on for you."

Kurt resisted.

He knew what was right and what was wrong and the way they were being treated was wrong. Surely she could see that. Yes, she could, but she also understood the basic truth that a rifle is more powerful than any number of words.

Her pleadings fell on deaf ears.

Down the stairs, he strode out into the plaza. He flung down his yellow star and proclaimed his defiance. "We are people – we are not dogs – we shall not be treated like vermin."

Inside, she listened and waited and then sobbed uncontrollably as she heard the unmistakeable crack of a rifle followed by the thump of a life extinguished.

WHY DID YOU?

Jeremy had won the Moon Beam Dinghy Regatta championship four times in a row. However, Kane was determined to end this winning streak – by any legitimate means, including the down right devious.

They both knew successful dinghy racing requires not just physical strength but also an unwavering determination to sail close to the wind – not just literally, but also with reference to the rules. Kane was aware that victory goes to those courageous enough to exploit every legal opportunity to obliterate the opposition. Especially in a championship contest.

On the penultimate day of the regatta, Kane began his mental campaign in earnest. "Well done yesterday, Jeremy. That was a close race but you absolutely had us. I have to admire your sail handling."

"You didn't do badly yourself. Your crew certainly knows how to handle that spinnaker. When you raise that super large bright red sail it's a danger sign for all other boats."

"Yeh. Miley loves raising and setting that sail. And it certainly lets us fly over the water. We nearly had you but we were a fraction too late. Actually, the other day you were about to tell me why it's called a spinnaker?" Kane knew full well why, but letting Jeremy feel superior might come in handy in the future.

"Apparently it came from a boat called the Spinx which hoisted a massive free floating sail during a race and people referred to it as *'Spinx's acre of sail'* and so the term stuck."

"Thanks, I always wondered. See you on the water this afternoon."

The ensuing race was a roller coaster. Kane and Jeremy kept swapping the lead as they went around each mark on the course. The spinnakers were hoisted, filled with wind and then hauled back down just in time before reaching the next mark.

Near the end of the race, Jeremy was only slightly in the lead when Miley did her best. In a flash, up went the big red spinnaker. It filled with wind and the boat fairly lifted out of the water and skimmed over the waves. From being 50 yards behind, Kane overtook Jeremy and won the race.

In the clubhouse, Kane added some more psychological pressure. "I know it seems stupid for me to help you, but from friend to friend, you've got to have your crew set the spinnaker faster. If he had, we'd never have caught you today."

Jeremy agreed. "I suppose you're right. Thanks. I'll have a word with Bobby. He's got to stop arguing – if I say up, then it's got to go up immediately."

With no hint of a smile Kane felt his campaign was succeeding. "That's the way, Jeremy. Bobby's got to respond without question."

Kane kept up the pressure, "I see from the scores that we're absolutely level. No one else can win the cup. Just one of us. So, who ever crosses the line first between the two of us wins the championship."

Jeremy smiled a confident smirk, "Yeh. But tomorrow all you'll see is our transom and we'll win the race and the championship again – making it five in a row. Just you watch."

Kane smiled back. "Not if Miley has anything to do with it you won't. See you tomorrow."

All week Kane had been studying the weather forecast and as predicted, finals day dawned with a strong wind. Not just strong but gusty and changeable. Although Jeremy and his crew were more suited to this type of weather, Kane had a plan taken straight from the book on gamesmanship.

The final race was again very close with Jeremy ahead on the final leg of the course. It was a now or never moment.

Kane went for it.

"Miley, we're going to raise the spinnaker."

"What? Are you out of your mind? You cannot be serious! The wind's in the wrong direction and far too strong. We'll capsize almost immediately before I can even set the sail."

"I know. But when you've raised it, I don't want you to let the wind get in the sail. Hold on to the sheets tightly. Fiddle with the sail as if something's wrong. Just keep the wind out of the sail. All we want is for Jeremy to see it going up."

Miley's face changed from a worried scowl to a cheeky grin. "Nice. I like it."

In the boat ahead Jeremy felt confident. With less than half a mile to go the championship was his. He had been turning back every few seconds to check if Kane was catching up. But this time, he was gripped with fear. He could see that big red spinnaker rising on Kane's boat and he knew Kane and Miley could easily overtake him unless he also responded by flying his spinnaker. He gave the fateful order to his crew, "Raise and set the spinnaker. Do it quickly."

So up went Jeremy's spinnaker. It filled with wind and … and over went the boat, capsizing with only a few hundred yards to go. Race lost!

Having seen Jeremy capsize, Miley knew exactly what to do and hauled down the big red sail as quickly as she could. It didn't need to fill with wind to do its work. Kane and Miley cheered as they crossed the finish line winners of the race and winners of the championship.

After Jeremy and his crew had been rescued, the two of them came charging up to Kane in the clubhouse, "I suppose congratulations are in order but why? Oh why did you raise your spinnaker? That wind was far too strong at that point. So why did you raise it?"

Kane smiled, "You're right – the wind was far too strong. So why did we do it? Simple —— because I thought you might respond and raise yours. And you did. Oops – wrong decision there, Jeremy – Tough luck. See you next year ... when we bring the cup back."

Author's Note

The event depicted at the end of this story did, in fact, occur basically as written. Although the person named in the story as Kane did not win the championship, the gamesmanship portrayed in this tale did happen during one of the Poole Week sailing regattas much to the annoyance of the other crew who fell for the ruse and capsized. They were not happy with Kane and back in the clubhouse they did genuinely ask *'Why did you?'*

Although devised by the crew on the water during a race in the 1980s, the ploy could have merited inclusion in the 1947 book by Stephen Potter entitled *'The Theory and Practice of Gamesmanship, or the Art of Winning Games without Actually Cheating'*.

THE LOTTERY OF LIFE

After sitting through an old episode of the Big Bang Theory, Tim finished his cup of tea and turned to his wife. "Before we turn in for the night, I'll just check the lottery numbers."

"You're not still buying those stupid things are you? Any way it's Tuesday and the Lotto isn't drawn on Tuesdays."

"You're right there, Sally, but it's the Euromillions I buy – not the Lotto. It has a much better payout."

"Yes and there's a good reason for that, Tim – there's much less chance of winning. Apparently it's just one in a hundred million."

"Actually it's worse than that. It's one in 139 million 838 thousand 160. Did you know you'd have to spend 349 million 595 thousand 400 pounds to guarantee winning?"

"It may come as a surprise to you, Tim, but we don't have that much. At the odds you just mentioned, why don't you just agree there's zero chance of winning and stop wasting our money."

"Why do I buy tickets? Because the odds aren't zero. As I said they're 139 million eight —"

"You told me that before and frankly that's as close to zero as makes no difference."

"Close – yes. But it's not zero and somebody wins – and it could be us."

"Yes it could and you know what? I could think what you're doing is sensible – but the probability of me thinking that has even lower odds."

Tim shrugged his shoulders and walked out of the room. He left Sally watching the news which Tim thought was an equally ridiculous waste of time.

During the frustrating minute it took for his ancient laptop to fire up, Tim took out his Euromillions ticket. With one click of a pre-programmed button, the screen displayed the Euromillions results. Being the archetypical optimist, Tim reached for his trusty lucky ball point pen – the one he always used for circling all the right numbers on his tickets. He hadn't used much ink from that pen – in fact often he used none.

Tonight, as per all previous such sessions, he began the ritual of the addicted – look at the number on the screen and then while speaking it out loud look at the ticket to see if it's there and circle it if lady luck has passed nearby.

"14 – hey – I've got one. … 22 – I've got that one as well – two numbers – at least I'll get a free ticket for the next draw. … 24 – and that one – three numbers? That may be enough for another ticket and a cup of coffee. … 27 – yep. This is getting unreal – I've never had four numbers before. … 33 – what – another? This is getting spooky and serious. Five correct numbers – that could be many thousands. Oh I'm looking forward to seeing Sally's face as she chews on her words – zero chance eh? Now for the lucky stars – oh my god! It's a 2 just like the ticket. Hold your breath kiddo as you check the last lucky star – 8."

Tim could hardly hold the lucky pen as he circled the seventh and final number on the ticket. He sat and stared at the full house on the ticket. With his heart going into overdrive, he looked at the prize value – £72,348,745.11 – certainly enough to justify having bought the ticket.

Once his heart rate had subsided back to near normal, Tim adopted a nonchalant attitude as he strode quietly back into the living room where Sally was channel hopping trying to find something interesting.

"Not find anything to watch, dear?"

"No – I thought I'd look while you were wasting your time."

"Well you might want to look at this pink paper I'm holding."

"Has clever clogs got two numbers again? What's that get you – a free ticket?"

"If I only had two numbers, it would. But I have more than that."

"Really? Let me see."

Tim handed her the ticket which showed all seven numbers circled. Sally went into a temporary catatonic state. Her eyes opened wide, her breathing became audible as she stayed sitting quite still. "Are you telling me – are you saying – does this mean millions?"

"Remember I said the odds are not actually zero and I said someone wins."

Sally kept staring at the ticket.

She then let out a moan, a groan, a horrific sound as she handed the ticket back to Tim. "You absolute fool, Tim. Look at the date. This is Tuesday, the day Euromillions is drawn, and this ticket is not for today – it's for last Friday – not today – last Friday. This is not a winning ticket. Oh how I hate you doing this to me. Why could you not do it correctly? You've really upset me."

Tim took the ticket back and looked carefully at it while Sally burst into tears.

He stood quite still as his eyes examined the ticket carefully. In a solemn tone he agreed with what she had said. "You're right, Sally. Oh so right. Today is Tuesday and this ticket is for last Friday."

Before Sally could berate him even more for upsetting her he spoke again in a soft whisper. "It's probably a good thing then that I checked this ticket against last Friday's numbers."

Author's Note

At the time of writing this tale, the Euromillions lottery was being drawn on Tuesdays and Fridays. The pattern was 5 numbers ranging from 1 to 50 and two lucky stars ranging from 1 to 12. As such the probability of winning is 1 in 139,838,160 or put another way 0.000000715 %.

NO LOGICAL REASON

There was no logical reason why Brody should not go to work that day. He was not ill. He had no dentist appointment. No holiday entitlement. He just felt he should not go. Call it a gut feeling or a premonition or whatever, but something was telling him —— *Don't go!*

As he lay in bed trying to understand why he had this feeling, Brody finally decided he was being silly. Although he was now going to be late, he dressed for work and set off. It would be better to be late rather than claim sick when he wasn't.

Anyway, he had a birthday present to give that day to the girl who sat at the next desk. They had gone on a few dates and things were looking good. He had chosen and carefully wrapped a turquoise silk scarf to go with her flowing red hair. Brody looked forward to seeing her radiant smile when she opened the present.

Normally the office began work by 8:30 but due to his late start, it would be at least nine before Brody would reach his final subway stop. But he never actually got there. At about 8:55, the subway train stopped a few stations early and everyone was told to evacuate quickly – something serious had happened.

When he reached street level Brody began shaking uncontrollably as he saw the North Tower of the World Trade Center engulfed in flames and thick black smoke. It was not just the very building where he worked but the very floor where he should have been that morning.

The very space where his red haired friend would now be enduring unimaginable fear – if she was even still alive.

Although Brody was never registered as a victim, the effect of watching the building collapse an hour later completely altered his life and destroyed his confidence. Within a month he left the horrific memories of New York behind and moved to the open spaces of Montana in an attempt to distance himself from the trauma of that day.

However, when his psychiatric counsellor told him shocks to the mind can take longer to heal than physical injuries, Brody knew exactly what she meant. Even now, more than twenty years on, he cannot go into a tall building without beginning to shake with fear and memory. He sometimes wonders how many others still suffer the same level of 9/11 survivor syndrome.

And how many others still keep an old, unopened birthday present as a reminder of what could have been.

PING

At the supermarket self-check out facility, Garath always made sure he scanned each item carefully as he hated getting that dreaded message, "Unexpected item in check out area." Doing it slowly also gave him time to listen to the reassuring ping as the machine acknowledged each of his purchases.

Scones – ping; clotted cream – ping; strawberry jam – ping. He was so absorbed in his own little world he almost failed to notice the lady at the next check out speaking to him.

"That looks like the makings of a cream tea. I can fully understand if you regard that as an *essential* purchase."

Garath looked up and was startled to see that the lady looked very familiar. It was hard to be sure, though, given the large COVID mask she was wearing over her nose and mouth and right up under her glasses. But her eyes were the give away – eyes he was sure he knew from the past.

Government lockdown regulations stipulated that one could only go shopping for *essential items*. His reply was, therefore, obvious, "Essential? Absolutely."

He smiled but then she could not see that through his surgical type blue COVID defences covering most of his face. But the slight lift and sparkle in his eyes that she had known so well in the past confirmed her thoughts. She knew that some say coincidences never happen but here she was in a supermarket standing beside a dear college friend she should never have lost contact with.

With an equally hidden smile she replied. "It's been a long time since we last met up." After all these years she knew his name but not so well she could remember it at that moment.

Her comment confirmed his feelings – it was her – if only he could recall – was she Kelly or Lil? Not a good idea to get it wrong. So in between the pinging of his purchases he settled for a neutral reply.

"Yes – far too long." He noticed her shopping items seemed rather sparse so added, "That doesn't seem much for the two of you."

"Two of us? You haven't heard? I was finally able to divorce that cheating bastard just before COVID lockdown. Apparently one of the last cases through the courts before they shut."

"So you've been on your own as well throughout this isolation? I can empathise – not pleasant being alone is it?"

Her brow furrowed slightly – it was all he could really see of her face as she mumbled through her mask. "But I thought … didn't you … weren't you getting married?"

"Almost. We lived together for a few years until last Christmas when Gary came by."

"Gary? Do I know Gary?"

Garath scrunched up his face which made his mask twitch like a set of whiskers. "No you wouldn't and frankly I don't want to recall either of them now. But he's more than welcome to her. After a while it became obvious we weren't compatible. I've been on my own since then."

At that point they both finished their pinging and made their payments using contactless cards in accordance with government guidance. But being contactless towards each other was not a priority in their minds. They continued their conversation as they walked out of the supermarket and stood close together at the road side. They were not really displaying any concern about adhering to some two metre anti-social distance guidance which Garath had discovered was being promulgated by a former government economist.

She enquired. "Shopping in the morning? Does that mean you're not working?"

With a slight shrug Garath replied. "Working? No. The company I was working for had to shut down due to lockdown regulations and guess what – it went bankrupt. So now no job and loads of time. And you?"

"During my disastrous marriage I worked for my ex, but that ended with the break-up. I'd planned to move back to Dorchester after the divorce and look for a job there but then along came – *'Stagnate at home; only go out for essential items'* which meant I couldn't go out looking for a job even if there was one, what with all the businesses shut. So – no, I don't have a job either."

Dorchester? That sparked a memory for Garath and he knew now that this was Kelly. He'd always had a fondness for her and had often wondered what had happened to her. Now he knew.

As they stood talking their upbeat mood was threatened by the drizzle that began to fall. Garath took the initiative. "Hey this is stupid standing here in the rain. I don't know what your schedule is but I've got time for a coffee. Do you?"

She nodded her head so they both hurried over to the cafe across the road. It was one of those places for which the incomprehensible government rules stipulated that you had to wear a mask when you ordered your food but you could take it off when you sat down. They ordered a latte and a cappuccino and sat down at a table in the corner fenced off from the rest of the world by a flimsy plexi-glass barrier. Garath knew this was not the most inviting environment but he was acutely aware the relevant government anti-COVID regulations did not include any sense of decorum, assuming they made any consistent sense at all.

They both removed their masks at the same time and stared at each other.

Garath was the first to speak. "Unless you've changed dramatically, now you've taken off your facial armour I'm thinking you're not the person I thought you were. You're not Kelly are you?"

This unknown but very attractive woman smiled back. "No. And without your medieval visor, I can see you're not Stephen, are you?"

"No – never been Stephen – always been Garath."

They both began to chuckle at this turn of events and were still giggling and joking about the mix-up when the waitress came by resplendent in black apron, black mask, a plastic visor and blue Nitrile gloves. She uttered an incomprehensible, "La – an – cap – no?" The girl's mumbles through her mask turned their mirth into outright laughter. Garath stopped long enough to confirm. "Yes that's ours."

So the waitress placed the order on the table and backed away quickly perhaps for fear of catching their contagious merriment. Government guidance said nothing about being allowed to laugh but did include the dictat that talking or singing loudly in restaurants was against the rules. And these two were certainly laughing dangerously loudly.

As they settled down, Garath resumed the conversation. "I can't really say I'm sorry to hear about a divorce between two people I didn't know. But the divorce is perhaps to my advantage as I guess it means you're probably free to sit and chat?"

"I sure am. And having just learned that Gary took who ever she was away from someone I've just met, leaving them all alone, I can see I'm not intruding. So – shall we start again? You said you're Garath? Well, handsome Mr Garath – I'm Tamsin, and by the way, I adore cream teas."

"Afternoon cream tea? Could do, but unless you've got other plans, might I suggest first a government sponsored lunch under the '*Eat out to help out'* hand out?"

Tamsin's face lit up. "Hey. If the chancellor wants to pay us to eat, it would be churlish of me to turn down such a thoughtful, deeply personal and considerate invitation. D'you have somewhere in mind? If not, I know a nice place in Swanage."

That lovely seaside town was over ten miles away and since Garath only had a bicycle, her suggestion could be awkward. "Swanage? D'you have a car?"

Tamsin pouted her lips and fluttered her eyelashes. "A girl's got to get something worthwhile from a divorce. So yes – a small open topped beamer."

Garath swallowed hard and nodded appropriately. "That'll do just fine, ma'am."

Then after a slight pause he added, "I think you'd agree, today seems to be masked in surprises."

Tamsin's face was all aglow as she responded. "Yep, but my Gran always said to me – 'Never ignore the unexpected'. But come on – drink up – if we're going to Swanage it's time to go."

"Yes boss. I'm ready." As he gulped down the remains of his latte, Garath mused to himself that Tamsin certainly qualified as – *Unexpected item in check out area.*

Author's Note

During the various COVID 19 *'lockdown'* periods in England, people were required to wear a mask in shops and while walking around a restaurant but once they sat down in the restaurant they were allowed to remove their mask.

During August 2020, the government had a scheme to help the hospitality industry whereby anyone buying a meal in a restaurant could claim back half the cost up to a limit of £10. The scheme was called *'Eat Out to Help Out'* and was used enthusiastically and extensively by the public with a total claim back of over £840 million. Since this vastly exceeded expectations, the government did not repeat the scheme.

A STRANGE PLACE

It is a strange place to be. John does not know how he got here – he only knows it is not the sort of place he would choose. The space is totally alien. He knows he does not belong here – he feels like a square peg jammed into a round hole but that implies a three dimensionality to this space and he isn't even sure he is not in two dimensional space.

But no – it has three dimensions as there are walls and a ceiling and a floor, all with a repugnant decor. The walls are a putrid shade of mottled chartreuse and the floor is off white with flecks of red.

He looks with interest at the flecks and realizes they are not paint. They are dripplings of dried blood. Human blood? Animal blood? Upon reflection, he decides animal blood, as the alternative is too stressful a conclusion. If it was human blood, was it his? If not, would he be next? So all told, this is not somewhere he wants to be.

But how did he get here? No doors or windows are visible and the ceiling looks solid. At that moment the floor starts rising, reducing the space he has.

"STOP." He yells but no one appears to hear.

No – he mustn't yell again as his shout has only increased the speed with which the floor is rising. His temperature increases. He can feel the sweat dribbling down his back and legs. Soon there is only room for him to lie flat and now the ceiling starts pressing down hard making breathing virtually impossible. His brain is screaming and searching for a way out.

At that point his basic survival instincts take over and with one great heave he throws off the heavy duvet and lays on the bed shaking and trembling from his near death experience dream.

STACEY

With her heart pounding so hard she can hear it in her ears, Stacey keeps running. Has she lost her pursuers? Oh no! She hears voices behind her. Two men puffing and wheezing.

"Come on Andy – we can catch her – she's not going to – get the better of us."

"We should – never have – let her – get away – you're right – she's bound to – tire soon."

But their words only spur Stacey on. She's going through the forest and looks behind. No sign of them. She keeps going when suddenly her left foot squelches into thick mud. She's afraid the mud may pull her shoe off.

She uses valuable time reaching down to ease her foot and shoe out of the mud. Then she hears them again.

"Look Andy – there she is."

Stacey has never run so fast as she does now. Adrenaline flows from the fear in her mind. *They won't catch me —— I won't let them.*

She is out of the forest now and sees some people ahead. If she gets to them, then it will be over. They won't be able to catch her in front of that crowd.

She runs through what looks like a small gate and trips. She falls to the ground with a groan. Her mind is spinning. *Will somebody speak to me —— please?*

And somebody does, "Well done Stacey. You're the first woman back and you've set a new course record. You've even beaten your husband Andy."

TAP TAP TAP

Hi – my name is Meldrum – Jared Meldrum – or at least that's what it was. I was born in 1897 on my parents' farm on the north shore of Lake Ontario. Well to call it a farm is rather stretching the normal meaning of the word. The land between Belleville and Toronto is not good for farming. The fields consist of thick, sticky, heavy clay soil with many rocks, both small and large which makes it virtually impossible to plough.

We had a few cows, some pigs and a scratching of chickens but it was always hard work. And muddy. You could not believe the mud – if it rained on Monday the soil was still ankle deep in oozy slimy mud on Friday. I left school when I was fifteen to help my parents eke out a living on this patch of bad land.

When that archie-dukie somebody got killed in 1914 in Europe and it meant Britain and Germany went to war, I saw my chance to escape without appearing to abandon my parents. *'Your King Needs You'* – how could a good upstanding country lad refuse such a call – it would be an honour to enrol. Oh, I have to admit, the thought of getting away from the mud was part of the appeal. Don't get me wrong. Mum always kept our house clean – boots off at the back door, change into clean jeans before you sit down, etc. But every day I knew I would have to go outside again to feed those damn pigs and that meant more mud.

I joined the Princess of Wales Own Regiment in Kingston. The training was hard but it was fun. The other lads in my platoon were also farm lads and we would tell each other tales about our life, about hunting foxes, about fishing and the fun of going into town for a barn dance. We knew we were going to fight in France and we were told French girls love dancing.

After a few months of bashing the square and learning to love our rifles, we were put on a big boat and when I say big, I mean BIG. We sailed out of, I think it was Quebec City, and started out across the ocean. I thought the captain must have lost his way 'cause the sailing went on for days and days. The only thing that changed was the size of the waves. Small waves meant you didn't feel quite as sick, large waves meant you not only felt sick, but you were sick. As a consequence, the toilets, or heads as they call them on a boat, had a rather obnoxious smell which meant if you went there and weren't yet feeling sick, you soon would be and nearly always were.

After an eternity, we landed in England. In rain. We were put in tents, some of which leaked a bit but at least the land stayed still which meant in a couple of days we lost that feeling of being sick. But very soon, a week at the most, we were put on a train and then into another boat. Sensing we were not overly thrilled, our sergeant called out, "You're off to the front, lads, so look smart."

Fortunately, the trip didn't last long and soon another train took us close to the front, whatever that meant. We then marched along carrying our packs on our back and singing – singing whatever came to our mind and frankly not very well, but we were in good spirits. We were off to beat the Hun at the Somme and show him that Canadians are tough.

And then came a rude shock. There were no barracks, not even tents, just trenches dug in the mud. I thought I'd seen mud at home, but this was real, first class mud. There was nowhere to get away from it. After a few days we learned not just the feel of mud but also the taste of mud. My boots soon had more mud on the inside than the outside and I thought my feet would rot. Apparently that had happened to some poor guys.

But the really bad thing was the annoying tap-tap-tap sound. I asked my sergeant what it was and he said it was the German machine guns. So I asked him, "What are they shooting at?"

He didn't answer directly. Instead he just put an old mud covered helmet on the end of a stick and held it up above the trench. Soon there was that tap-tap-tap. When he brought the helmet back down, there were three bullet holes in it. He then turned to me. "You asked – what are they shooting at? Any helmet —— preferably with someone's head inside it."

Innocently, I then commented. "But I thought you said we climb out of these trenches and march towards the Hun. Won't he be shooting at us?"

"That's where the generals come in, lad."

"What? The generals come here?"

"No – no. They're safely back at head quarters, fifty or so miles back. But they know what's happening and tell us when it's safe to climb out. You'll know when it's safe – we'll be blowing our whistles and you can climb out and run towards the Hun. He won't be expecting us so it's ok. Remember, when you hear the whistle, the generals have said it's safe."

The very next day at seven in the morning just after we'd drunk our mud and tea mixture, the whistles shrilled right along the trenches. We looked at each other and commented, "If the generals are saying it safe, then let's go and get Fritz and his noisy gun."

I climbed out of the trench with my rifle at the ready, bayonet fixed. I began running towards the enemy when, tap-tap whiz.

Apparently my disfigured dying body was already mired in the mud before the third bullet could make yet another hole in my helmet.

DATA GATHERING

Part 1

"I'm having another. How about you, Lenora? Gin and tonic again?"

Graham picked up his empty pint and wandered over to the bar. This pub was one of his favourites – a cosy country-style pub. The discussion of the younger set perched on the bar stools was being overshadowed at intervals by the discussion in the far corner on roses – black spot, green fly, mildew and all manner of sure-fire cures. Living in a bed and breakfast, Graham regarded the pub as his living room – a place to meet and make friends. He had met Lenora here that very evening.

"Here you are. I poured all the tonic in – is that OK? You were telling me what you did."

Lenora replied in a vague, question-stopping manner that she just interviewed people. Nothing fancy, rather dull at times, data gathering could be another way of putting it. Graham was also in the data gathering business, but he chose not to tell her everything about his work.

"At the moment I'm a contract programmer."

"That's not like being a contract killer, is it?"

"No – not exactly a contract killer, but that's an interesting thought." What a funny woman. Contract thief maybe, but not a contract killer.

"Contract programmers work for a customer for a specified period under short term contracts. We help with whatever they want – program design, coding, testing."

He mulled over the last word – testing. Yes, testing provided him with the opportunities he needed.

She asked, "Do you specialize?"

"Yes, I suppose I do – mostly financial institutions. You know how it is from your interviewing – one contact leads to another and at the moment I'm working with the money sharks. It's an awful term but that's what they call themselves. ... Time? It's just gone ten."

"I'm sorry, Graham, but I have to dash. Will we see each other again?"

"If you want to."

"Of course I do. I'd hardly have asked you if I didn't."

As Graham looked at her eyes, he noticed them soften slightly and her left eyebrow lift a twitch. In response, he inclined his head almost imperceptibly and thought to himself – she really means it.

"Thursday? 8 o'clock? ... Fine. See you then. Bye, Graham."

Because Graham's job took him all over the country, he did not have a home base or a steady relationship. As a consequence, he had learned to meet people and form friendships quickly. Lenora had responded warmly to his chatter and he was looking forward to seeing her again.

Graham did not spend the time between their parting and meeting in idle work or dreaming. No. His job demanded his full attention. His very freedom depended upon it. In simple terms, Graham was a freelance thief. The objects of his attention, however, were not tangible items such as silver or jewellery. Graham stole data and sold it to unscrupulous customers.

He had told Lenora the truth when he said he specialized in the financial area. Credit lists, personal loans, debit card details, account numbers. These were all targets of his quest for data. Graham gained access to such data under the guise of testing the computer systems.

"Test data should be realistic. I don't just mean in terms of values but also in the spread and pattern of messages. Generated data just isn't the same. It's artificial and the test results are also artificial. Real data – real results. Generated data – unreliable results."

When pushing this line with a client, Graham could almost begin believing it himself. Some clients resisted his insistence and only supplied unrealistic generated data. But he could not sell fictional credit lists – they were as much use as last week's weather forecast.

The current job involved salary and bonus payments and the computer manager was being stubborn. This was awkward for Graham since he had already arranged a buyer for the data.

"Yes, Graham, there's no need to go over the points again. I agree with the principle but is our office security adequate to protect such sensitive data? Even our own managers only have restricted access. We really can't have such data circulating in the office."

Eventually a compromise was reached which Graham found comical in the extreme. He would work offsite for a couple of weeks and they would send the live test data direct to his offsite location – delivered in a security van no less. He was able to examine the data and extract what he needed with no one suspecting anything. He had done a quick check and the cross index tables pointed to the right people at the right kind of salary. Superb. He finished the testing as required. However, he also made copies of the data which he then sold to his 'other' client. This customer was not one of Graham's usual contacts but came with proper credentials – green ones and many of them.

On Thursday when he met up again with Lenora they talked endlessly, exploring and mapping each other's responses.

Normally Graham's approach to women was more direct, but Lenora was different – he actually enjoyed her company. He suggested walking her home for coffee.

"Sorry, Graham, we can't." And she was genuinely sorry. "I live with my mother and she disapproves of virtually everything. It wouldn't be a good idea. But perhaps you have a jar of coffee at your place?"

"Also no can do. I live in a B&B and they have stupid rules about guests – none allowed. Perhaps I should move?"

His remark was met with a slight tilt of her head and a raising of her left eyebrow – that enticing little move he had noticed the first time they met.

He questioned her reason. "You say your mum disapproves of —"

"My friends, my hobbies, even my work."

Graham could understand this. She had not been forthcoming about her job – perhaps she was also in a dubious line. With her quick wit and enquiring mind he could easily visualize her operating some insurance scam. *'Gathering data'* she had said the first time they met – they obviously had a lot in common. But she had not pried about his job so he decided he would respect her silence and not enquire further about her work. At least not yet. But he was foreseeing a workable liaison, in more ways than one. With his contacts and her skills, they could pull off some fantastic scams and jobs.

Over the next few weeks they continued to meet only in the pub. This was most uncharacteristic of Graham. Normally he would have moved on and found someone more willing – someone with an apartment where they could spend the night. But Lenora – she was different. The warmth and passion in their end of evening embraces after the pubs closed convinced Graham that she was worth concentrating on. He frequently thought of her when his mind should have been on his work.

Graham's contract changed and he began working for another company – Caledonian Credit. This company processed credit applications and presented new opportunities with new data to sell. His interest lay not in the good ratings but more in the rejected ones. Some of his customers made a very profitable business lending money at exorbitant rates to people whose loan applications had been rejected by others. But first another discussion with management.

"We've always used small test packs that we make up as needed. Why all your concern about *'real'* data? It'll take ages to produce and I can't spare anyone for it."

"Have you examined your test packs and compared them against the live runs? … No? … I suspect you'll find they aren't worth keeping. I think we're actually agreeing with each other. To have an analyst or anyone else prepare made up data is an expensive use of your resources. I mentioned at our last meeting I've developed a data extraction program which I think you'll find saves effort not only in the long run but right now – this week – today."

"Graham. I don't like this situation at all, but perhaps I'll have to go along with your suggestion. To keep these delivery dates we need test data and I have no one available to prepare it. How much is your software going to cost me?"

Graham would gladly have installed it with no charge. The program had some special extraneous *'work'* and *'sort'* files which were used for collecting the more interesting items of data. However, if the client was willing to pay to be robbed, who was Graham to stop him?

By the time he went to the pub later that week to meet Lenora, the program was installed and producing useful saleable data. Graham was almost relaxed about the business.

And almost careless.

"Come on, Graham, before I dash off to catch my bus, tell me how selling a program for three hundred could make you so happy. There must be more to it than just the money."

"There is Lenora – by God there is. But I can't tell you yet 'cause there are some details to tidy up."

"Next time we meet? I want to know what makes you so excited. Is she dark, good looking, taller than me?"

"Cut the teasing, Lenora. It's not another girl and OK, I'll tell you next week when we meet. I'll tell you all about it. You might even find it interesting."

Graham's happiness had been infectious and Lenora went off in a cheerful mood with a whimsical thought. She enjoyed Graham's company – he made her feel relaxed and secure. He did not attempt to force himself on her and she liked that. With the problems of her mother and his bed and breakfast, she began dreaming about them perhaps going away together for a weekend somewhere.

Detective Constable Lenora Scott was still cheerful the following morning as she reported for work at her police station. Since they were in the middle of a major full time investigation, she decided to check with Graham first before asking for weekend leave.

Part 2

The following evening, in another part of town, the subway station was deserted.

Graham had received a message to be at this station at 11:30. He had walked from one end of the platform to the other and there was no one else around. At least no one he could see. But then he heard them — two people.

There was the steady footstep of a heavy man. Between the metallic ring of each footstep, Graham could hear the quieter sound of a pair of trainers. These had a slower rate indicating a taller person.

Eleven thirty it was and he was rapidly regretting his decision to meet these people. Especially when he heard their voices.

"… so tell me again. Why are wees only roughin' him up?"

"Look, I told yah, didn't I? He sold PJ some duff data and the word is he has to pay for it … physically. 'member as kids how Mum used to scold us for fightin' – God she'd be proud of us now. Guess you could call us 'Brother's in Arms'. So, we're just gonna hurt him enough to teach him a lesson."

Graham had heard enough.

"OK. But how d'you know he's here?"

"Look. We sees him come down here, right? There have been no trains, right? So he's here. PJ's arranged it."

"Where? I can't see him." They had arrived on the platform and the question brought a growl from the other man.

The two brothers always worked as a pair. They had done so since their primary school days when, for a fee, they *protected'* the other kids' pocket money. From there they had graduated to bootlegging and betting which had brought them to the attention of more organized crime.

They were inseparable and had made a solemn vow to each other – in the event of either of them being killed, the other would avenge his death with the death of the person responsible. They acted as enforcers for PJ and right now the instructions were merely for a roughing job. But the victim was nowhere to be seen.

"What? He must be down here. Come on. Let's search the platform and find this git. He ain't gonna pull a fast one on us."

They searched in every corner and behind every pillar but to no avail. Graham was underneath the platform edge praying for a train and planning alternative escape strategies. Just to add an element of excitement, he was contemplating the live rail with its multi-thousand volts only inches away from his nose.

When the train finally arrived, Graham could still hear the brothers searching. Under the cover of the platform edge, he crawled to the end of the platform stairs and waited, looking at the train guard. As the guard's hand brought the whistle to his mouth, Graham ran – ran up the stairs, ran along the platform and ran into the first open door.

Foiled.

They were waiting for him in that carriage. Within the ninety five seconds between stops, they pulverized Graham into a moaning, gut clutching, bleeding hulk. His nose would never be quite the same but his eyes would recover within days.

While administering this attack, they had explained PJ Mottram's displeasure at being sold useless data. Graham readily agreed to effect the proposed solution.

"PJ says he wants some good data this time. You un'erstand?"

Graham disliked the tall man's use of the word *'understand'* – it appeared to be a cue for the short one to kick him. Un'erstand – thunk.

"So where are you workin' now?"

Graham could barely mumble the answer, "Caledonian Credit."

"Eh – I don't un'erstand." – thunk.

"Caledonian Credit."

"Oh, now I un'erstand." – thunk.

"We'll call you soon so yous better have de stuff ready. If PJ don't like de data, I mights have to turn nasty. You un'erstand?" – thunk.

Although the short fat one laughed, Graham failed completely to see the humour in the tall man's exit line. Nasty? His shirt was already quite red enough – they had his full attention. Graham waited on the train for another couple of stops, then left and took a taxi home.

Lenora! He was due to see Lenora in a few days. But looking like this? What could he say? How could he explain it? One thing for certain – he could not ignore it, especially with his face looking like a badly bruised apple.

He had agreed to tell her about his work but not quite so dramatically. He was unsure how she would react but was confident she would understand. After all, he mused to himself, almost everybody does a bit of office pilfering only he was just a bit more organized – or was it careless?

Thursday arrived and as agreed, they met in the pub. In a dark corner of the pub. Her look of genuine concern and expression of warmth toward him made Graham feel that it was almost worthwhile. However, he knew he would change his mind when it came to shaving the following morning.

"Before you say anything, Lenora, it's not as bad as it looks and I probably deserved it."

During her time in the police force, she had seen such cases before and knew it was a professional job. But she found her training in being cool and dispassionate in such situations was hard to apply. This was different. This was Graham. Some one she knew and liked. Her Graham. The man she was dreaming of spending a weekend with.

"I sold a *'friend'* some items. It turned out they were defective and he was marginally displeased."

"Displeased? You surprise me. Come on, Graham, what's going on? If these are your *'friends'* as you put it, you've got a serious problem you've not told me about. I might be able to help."

"Help? No girl. This isn't something you could help with, dear, but thanks for the offer. And yes you're right – I do have another side to me. I sell data."

"What do you mean *'sell data'* – to who?"

"To whoever will pay – I'm not fussy."

"I'm confused, Graham, I thought you worked with computers. And now you say you sell data. What are you trying to tell me?"

"I do work with computers. I just kind of sell some of the data I come across during my work. You know – things can fall off the back of a truck? Well sometimes data seems to fall off the back of the computer and I – well – pick it up kind of like.

That's all. What I mean is I've access to sensitive data and I just kind of take a copy and sell it."

"Don't you mean you steal it?"

"That's a pretty strong word, but I suppose some people might think of it that way. But I don't deprive them of their data such as stealing jewellery – I just sell a copy of the data. Nothing is actually removed – they don't even know it's been copied. In legal terms I don't deprive them of their data so it's not like theft."

Lenora's thoughts were confused. Why had she fallen for a thief? Why Graham? The more they had seen each other, the stronger her feelings were for him. But she could not condone his actions. The stealing he indulged in was wrong – illegal. It was the type of activity she spent her working hours investigating and prosecuting.

Graham sensed a slight change in her mood. "I'm for another drink. You too?"

She nodded and as he went to the bar she tried to make sense of her predicament. Try though she might, Lenora could not arrive at an acceptable solution. She could not now tell him what she did but equally she could not ignore what he had said. And she could not ignore how she felt for him.

"Sorry, Lenora, they've already closed the bar. Time to go I guess."

As they walked outside, Lenora continued to express her concern.

"Thanks anyway. But what are you going to do about these people, Graham? You can't just ignore them."

"It's in hand already. They presented me with a proposal and I accepted."

"Graham, the more you tell me the worse it gets. Was it *'an offer you couldn't refuse'* by any chance?"

"Yeh, in a sort of way. They want more data – good data this time. So I made great noises about my current access to sensitive data and they were interested."

"You're a fool. They'll do it again and again. You won't be free of them. You should have said no to their plan."

"Lenora, that's easy to say standing here outside a cosy pub. Try saying that with a fist in your face and a boot in your stomach. He offered me a way out and I took it. All I have to do is supply lists from my current job."

"But how? Oh, Graham, I don't like this one bit."

"What am I supposed to do? Call in the police? Dear Mr Constable, me fence has beaten me up for passing on useless stolen articles."

Mentally Lenora corrected that to *'Dear Miss Constable'* but she kept quiet. She found the situation overbearing. She liked Graham – she had even thought she might be falling in love with him. But she also liked her career. It was permanent – he might be only temporary. She knew she would have to take the initiative.

"Graham. I'm being serious. You can't just let them get away with it."

"Look at my face, Lenora. A close look. I AM being serious. You don't just push PJ Mottram around. He's big."

PJ Mottram. The mention of that name frightened Lenora. Down at the station, she had been investigating him and his companies for over a year but it had been impossible to tie him into any of the accidents and fatal injuries that seemed to occur to his acquaintances.

But that was not what frightened her. She knew that PJ Mottram owned Caledonian Credit where Graham was working. Graham had unwittingly agreed to sell PJ his own data after blatantly stealing it from him. Displeased? Murderous would be more appropriate.

As she rode home on the bus, Lenora began formulating a plan.

When she approached her boss the following day his response was as expected. "Irregular. Highly irregular."

The head of CID in the local police station paced around the war room muttering into his chin. He then turned to her. "You cannot be serious. Are you sure it is the same person, Lenora? PJ Mottram?"

"Yes. And next time it won't be his lackeys. My contact is to meet directly with PJ."

"Are you free to tell me how you obtained this information – or is that an indiscreet question?"

"The latter, sir. The info is good and open, the source is good but closed. I know it's irregular but we've been working on this case for ages waiting for a break. We have one now – so let's use it."

"Before I can authorize your request, go over your plan once more – I have to satisfy the chief."

Part 3

The following week, Lenora and Graham met for dinner. Graham's battered face was semi-respectable again and in celebration they were having a special meal at a small candlelit Italian restaurant – her idea. Much though Graham would have liked the evening to end more romantically, they both knew he had an appointment later that evening.

"Looking at the frown on your face, anyone would think you were going to this meeting, Lenora – not me."

"I'm worried."

"Perhaps I shouldn't go. Perhaps I should say I'm sick or drunk or something like that."

"Oh no." The rapidity of her answer startled even Lenora. Given the plans she and the inspector had made, he must go. "I mean they'll only hound you and chase you and I'm concerned about the plan."

Lenora had not meant to use that word – plan. She hoped Graham would not attach any significance to what she had said – vain hope.

"What plan? All I'm doing is just going to meet this guy. That's hardly a plan."

"I'm just concerned, that's all."

That part was correct. Lenora was concerned that Graham follow the plan even if he didn't know there was one. She was also genuinely concerned for his safety – the whole plan was a risk.

In other parts of the town, other people were also making plans.

"I know, I know. Normally I go up to the loading platform and you two do the job down below. But this time you go up, Alex, and cover me and I'll do the talking. I want this guy myself."

"PJ. I don't think it's wise."

"That's your problem. You don't think – period. I said I'm going to do it and that's what I'm doing."

"PJ, I hear there could be…."

"You've started hearing as well. A right little Einstein, eh? Well if you can hear, then listen good – I am going. I am going to meet this snivelling Graham or whatever his name is, myself. You'll be upstairs as backup but I'll do it. For heaven's sake – you two can't have all the fun. This guy's spittin' in my face so I'll take him out personally. OK? … Now let's get going."

As PJ and the two brothers went off in their car, coffee was being served at the dinner for two.

"I don't want to push you, but aren't you cutting it a bit fine?"

Graham was feeling jittery and responded in like manner. "Lenora – slow down a pace and stop fretting. I'll do the worrying."

"I just don't want you to get hurt."

"Remember my face? What do you think that was? Make-up? It hurt and it still does. To put it bluntly, I'm stalling 'cause I'm afraid. I hear PJ carries a shooter and I really don't want to go."

Lenora stared at her coffee. She had not been prepared for the possibility that Graham might know this and was wondering how it might affect her plans.

"What's with you, girl? You've been peering into your coffee for ages and not listening. I said I'm going now."

Silently she leant forward and kissed him. Softly on the lips with her eyes wide open and moist.

"Graham, please – be careful. No matter what happens, please remember – I care and I'll always be thinking of you."

As he drove off in the taxi, he thought about her last words – they almost sounded like goodbye.

But Graham was not the first to arrive at the arranged meeting place. That honour went to the special armed response unit. Graham was not even the second.

PJ's car had been monitored as it drove on to the deserted land. There had been a large warehouse on the site but it had been demolished and left as a pile of rubble to avoid land taxes. Around the perimeter were derelict buildings, some in the ancient Dutch style with loading windows on the upper floors. Everywhere there was broken glass and gaping doorways. It was one of PJ's favourite venues.

"You know where I normally go. Take the rifle but just cover me. As I said, I'll do it this time. But if I miss, you take him out. Graham's death'll be a lesson to everyone. He thinks he can steal from me and sell me my own data? I'm taking him out. He'll be gone. Finished. Got it?"

The taller brother opened the car door and jogged over to the building on the south side. The moon would be behind him giving him an excellent view from the fourth floor loading bay. He was still climbing the stairs when Graham's taxi arrived.

Eleven o'clock they had said. He was early. As agreed, the taxi drove off and parked around the corner leaving Graham in the still darkness clutching the package of computer discs and printouts. He twitched alarmingly as the sound of breaking glass came from one of the buildings on the south side only to be followed by the squeal of a cat. The tall man had practiced that sound for hours for just such mishaps but he was now in place.

As were the hunters, in the same south building and on the ground. To catch PJ directly was a trophy worth pulling out the stops for. The tall brother had almost bumped into two of them but was too preoccupied to notice.

The distant church bells announced the time. Graham counted – nine, ten, eleven. And then other churches echoed back. The interplay seemed to go on forever. And then the silence returned.

The short brother whispered. "Hey, PJ. Shall I call him? Get his attention?"

"No. Let him sweat a bit more. Let him walk about some more cause it's the last walking he'll do."

PJ chuckled and his short fat companion chuckled as well. Finally, PJ flashed the car headlights twice, called out to Graham and turned on the full glare of headlights and fog lamps.

"Graham! Stay there. This is PJ. Is the data in that package?"

"Yes."

"The data from Caledonian Credit?"

"Yes!"

"The data you have stolen from Caledonian Credit?"

Graham was becoming very agitated – why all these questions?

"Yes, it's the credit lists from Caledonian Credit. What's the problem?"

With a dark growl PJ shouted back. "Your problem is – I own Caledonian Credit!"

Before Graham could fully appreciate the significance of his predicament he heard a woman's voice yelling – a voice he knew well, "Get down, Graham. Get down!"

Dazzled by the light and startled by the voice, he turned, stumbling on the uneven ground just as the first shot grazed his leg. He fell into a hollow and was now out of the light beam and could not be seen by PJ.

As the tall man in the loading bay took aim at Graham, he heard footsteps in the hall behind. Turning back, he fired into the darkness and his shots were returned. He took one step back, two steps back, three steps – but the platform did not extend that far and he tumbled down – his screams only stopping as he smashed on to the broken brick and glass below. The screaming stopped.

They might have charged PJ with attempted murder, but you cannot charge a corpse.

At the sight and sound of his tall brother tumbling to his death, the short brother began shouting at PJ.

"Dat was me brother, PJ. Me brother! You should've been on dat platform, not Alex. They'd 'ave shot you, not Alex. You should've left it to us – but no you had to do it your way. Your great plans killed me brother. You're responsible and you knows what that means. Alex an' I made a promise – and now you have to pay."

The fat man's rage was reflected in the frenzy of his knife attack on PJ. The knife went in and out like a jig saw. No mercy, no life. He was still butchering PJ when the armed response unit encircled the car.

Off in the darkness Graham was protesting unsuccessfully to another policeman.

"I tell you someone tried to shoot me. Why can't you stop talking and listen to what I'm saying?"

"I'm not listening 'cause I'm telling you. I'm telling you that you were out for a walk, you fell over and you hurt yourself. That was the first message from Lenora. The second…."

"Lenora? You know Lenora? Lenora Scott?"

"Of course I do. Everyone at the station knows D.C. Scott."

Lenora? A detective constable? A bloody policewoman? Graham felt his stomach tighten as he recalled the conversations they'd had, the questions she'd asked, his revelations. He almost did not hear the second message.

"She asked me to tell you that you should concentrate on something milder – like stock control systems – somewhere in the midlands or perhaps Scotland. Do you understand?"

The word 'understand' caused Graham to flinch – bad word.

"I think I do. Perhaps my leg's not that badly injured. Perhaps I just fell over. Perhaps I'll just go home now."

"You do that."

And he did. Fortunately, the taxi was still waiting for him around the corner and as Graham climbed in, he thought of Lenora. A snoop – she had called her work *'data gathering'*. What had he told her – would she come and arrest him – but she had no evidence. There were no finger prints – nothing was actually missing – anyway, the victims would deny it. There was nothing to trace. Perhaps that was why she let him go.

But then why had she called out just before the shot? It had saved his life. And her words of goodbye? And the kiss?

As the true explanation began dawning, Graham thought he would call her and explain. No, upon reflection, he would write to her. No, he couldn't do that either. He bit his lip as his eyes went wet and he realized his only real option was to update his CV and move on quietly without a word.

Never before had anyone cared that much for him – and he had to walk away without even saying goodbye. She had to become just a memory.

Still in the taxi, Graham began to assess the true cost of his data gathering activities – was the price too high in every way? He saw now that fate was handing him a second chance – take it, stop what he was doing and live – or – ignore this second chance and continue his activities and …

The decision was simple – Graham knew that fate did not deal out third chances.

ON THE TRAIN TO CARLISLE

As Roscoe stood up in the train he asked the lady opposite him, "Can you look after my things while I get a coffee?"

"Sure, no problem."

"Can I get you one? Coffee? Tea? What would you like?"

Susie did not normally accept such invitations from people she didn't know but in the train this was hardly a risk. She was, after all, agreeing to look after his things and she could do with a drink.

"White coffee, please; one sugar, thanks. By the way, I'm Susie, Susie Trendle."

"Roscoe Fernsbay and I'll be right back with the coffees."

When he had boarded the train, Roscoe noticed the reserved seat on the other side of the table was empty. The occupant would be boarding at another station which meant he was able to spread out his books and laptop on the table. Although the report for his client was finished, there was always other work to attend to. His concentration was interrupted at the next station by the person who had reserved the seat opposite.

Roscoe looked up and noticed a very attractive lady, about his age with strawberry blonde hair and an endearing smile that wrapped around her face. Thinking of the long journey ahead, he admitted to himself, *this is preferable to an old man with a sneeze and a snore*. But he was not really interested – his relationship with his partner Anthea was becoming serious and they were making plans for the summer.

Susie was heading north to visit her mother. She always did this in January ever since her Dad passed away. It was only for a couple of days so she was travelling light with just a small case and a large book. When taking a train, her preference was always to reserve a window seat with a table so she could relax with space.

But today, the table in front of her reserved seat was completely covered with this man's books and papers. She was about to ask him if he could give her some room but before she could do so, he gathered up his documents and apologized.

She didn't say anything, but Susie was impressed – *A considerate gentleman no less. A rather rare breed, especially in one who looks more like a model than a businessman.* She was reminded of the comment her friend Tanya kept making, "*Just 'cause you've ordered your meal doesn't mean you can't look at the menu.*" He was certainly a menu item but she was happy with her engagement to Terry.

And so they had sat in silence until Roscoe had become thirsty and asked her to look after his things.

He returned soon from the train kiosk with two coffees along with packages of biscuits and shortbread, "Travelling far?"

Susie thanked him and chose the shortbread. "Visiting my mother in Carlisle. And you?"

"I'm visiting a client in Penrith. I'm a systems analyst but you don't want to hear about that. Yourself?"

"I'm studying to be a translator. Terry, my fiancé, is being posted to Berlin and I thought being a translator could be useful – perhaps get a part time job there."

"Germany? Funny how the world works. Anthea, my lady, comes from Hanover."

Having established that both of them were otherwise attached, the conversation flowed easily without overtones or awkwardness. They spoke of their interests and hobbies and found much in common. Two cups of coffee and sandwiches later, they were still absorbed in conversation and laughter. So absorbed that they had not noticed either the passage of time or the change in the weather.

Or the fact the train had stopped with no station in sight – just snow all around with a strong billowing blizzard. That is until they heard the announcement over the tannoy. "I regret to announce that the snow drift ahead is too deep. The train will be stopped here until it can be cleared. We will update you with any change. We apologize for the inconvenience."

Susie laughed, "Have you noticed – they always apologize for the inconvenience when they don't really mean it?"

"From the sound of it, I guess we're here for a while. Is that a problem for you?"

"No. I'll just call Mum to tell her the train's delayed."

Susie rummaged in her bag but when she finally pulled her phone out she scowled, "No coverage!"

Roscoe looked at his phone, "I've got reception – do you want to use mine?"

"I couldn't ask you for that."

"You didn't ask. I offered."

"If you're sure you don't mind, thanks. I'll be quick!"

"Hey – take as long as you like – I'm not going anywhere."

"No – I suppose not."

He watched, she dialled and Mum answered. "Hi Mum, it's Susie … no I haven't changed number, my phone's dead and Roscoe has lent me his … no, Roscoe is not a new boyfriend – we are just sitting opposite each other on the train … yes we're still on the train – that's why I'm phoning you. The train is stuck in snow and we don't know when it will get to Carlisle … Yeh, I'll call you when we know … No, Mum, I really don't think Roscoe is dangerous … got to go now … love you too … and yes, I'll be careful, bye."

As she handed back the phone, Susie quipped, "Sorry – I should've asked you – are you dangerous? Are you going to run away with me under your arm?"

It was probably only a second or two but Susie felt he was taking a long time to answer. He raised his eyebrows and gazed into her eyes, "I am not sure. Was that a question or an invitation? But either way I think my Anthea and your Terry may have views on that."

"Oh yes, I'd forgotten about them." And she had.

Susie was definitely warming to this travelling companion and felt it was reciprocal. Which was a good thing because after more hours of friendly chatter they noticed that it was dark outside, the snow was deeper, the wind stronger and the carriage much colder. Even with her coat on, Susie was beginning to shiver.

Roscoe noticed, "You look cold – I've got a spare fleece in my case – do you want it?"

"Oh, but my Mum said to beware of the dangerous Roscoe! — But yes, if you really don't mind – I am very cold."

After Roscoe extracted the fleece from his case and Susie pulled it on, he looked at her with a smile that helped warm at least her heart. "Looks much better on you than it ever has on me."

Two more hours and the tannoy burst into life again, "Sorry to announce we will not be able to move the train until morning and the kiosk is now closed. We would also like to apologize for the reduced heating. If you have any coats or blankets, we suggest you wrap up."

"Roscoe, I don't suppose you have a blanket in your case as well, do you?"

"No, but I have a warm duffle coat."

"But you'll need that."

"Yeh, but, and please understand this is purely in the interest of survival, we could share it as a blanket if you sat over on this side."

"Of course. Purely in the interest of survival. And talking of sharing, I always take Mum a fruit cake. It's in my case and since the kiosk is now closed, d'you want to share it? ... Shall we eat it now?"

After they both devoured the cake, Susie moved over to the other side of the table, snuggled up under the duffle coat and rested her head on his shoulder. She felt a shiver tingle down her spine. It wasn't a shiver of cold and she tried to ignore it. But she knew this felt much better than it ever did with Terry. In spite of the cold, they were soon both asleep, curled up together to keep warm.

They awoke from their dream filled sleep when the train lurched and started to move. Roscoe was the first to talk. "This next station is mine."

"Pity. But hold on – you'll need your fleece back."

"No. You're still cold. You keep it. Anyway I don't want to try explaining to Anthea why my fleece now has a whiff of your perfume and is covered in blonde hairs."

As Roscoe stood up to leave, Susie spoke with a slight tear in her eye. "Ships passing in the night? Take care, Roscoe, you're one in a million." And she planted a soft kiss on his cheek. That was not where she wanted to kiss him but there were others to think of.

Over the next few months Roscoe often thought about his fleece and wondered if Susie still had it. Although they had not exchanged any contact details, Roscoe still had her mother's number on his phone. But he was not going to upset her engagement so he just consoled himself with the memory of that snowy train trip.

But he was not the only one who thought about the fleece. Susie could not bring herself to wash it – would that wash away the memory of him? And she didn't want that to happen. The memories had grown into dreams – dreams which always stopped with the harsh reality of Roscoe and Anthea.

Her friend Tanya was getting married in the spring and Susie became involved in the wedding preparations. Although Tanya's sisters would be the bridesmaids, Susie took an active role. She was helping to arrange the seating plan for the wedding dinner. It was fun until she found an entry in the groom's side of the guest list – 'Roscoe and Mrs Fernsbay'.

So Anthea had won – but then Roscoe had never pretended or acted otherwise. It could be awkward meeting him again but at least she could make sure she was not sitting at the same table as the two of them. Somehow, the fun had gone out of this wedding.

On the big day, she saw him standing alone and crept up behind him.

"I still have the fleece."

Roscoe recognised the voice, spun around, took one look and gave Susie a hug. He knew he shouldn't have but she was even more than he remembered. And she didn't appear to be objecting.

At that point an elderly woman appeared and enquired, "Roscoe dear, who is this ravishing blonde you are hugging?"

Roscoe replied. "Mum, this is Susie. I might have mentioned her to you. Once or twice."

Susie's eyes opened wide, "Mum? Did you just say Mum? Are you the Mrs Fernsbay on the guest list? I thought it was Anthea – is she not here?"

"No! Anthea sat in a Ferrari and drove off with its owner – a city stock broker. No, Anthea is well and truly gone. I'm on my own now. Talking of that, where's your fiancé?"

"I found out Terry was engaged to another girl at the same time so out he went! And it wasn't in the recycling bin."

At this point, Roscoe's mother spoke up.

"If you two can let me get a word in edgewise, who did the seating plan?"

Susie replied with a puzzled voice. "I did, why?"

"Because, silly girl, you have me sitting beside my son and it's obvious it would be much better if the two of you were sitting together – again – I understand you sit well together. So

I'm trading seating places with you – no argument! Anyway that means I meet some other people. Agreed? … Good."

"Roscoe. Is your mother always this bossy?"

"Yeh she is — but she's nearly always right."

Susie smiled, "Good. I like her already."

She then turned to Mrs Fernsbay and spoke with words which conveyed more than just gratitude, "Thanks —— Mum."

Author's Note

The train from southern England to Carlisle in the north goes over high ground just before it reaches Penrith. The weather in that area is often unpredictable and in winter the train can be held up for hours by unexpected snow drifts.

BEST DAY OF THE WEEK

On Wednesday Martha, Aiden and Janice were propping up the coffee dispenser trying to decide which day of the week each thought was best.

Aiden favoured Mondays as he went to the gym Monday evenings. However, from the look of his powerful physique the others were sure he had more than one intensive work-out per week.

Martha favoured Sunday. "It's the one day of the week when Owen brings me an early morning cuppa. Sometimes he makes the tea too strong but I don't complain. He might take that as a sign he should stop."

Janice queried her choice. "Is that the best you can do? A cuppa in the morning?"

"If you lived with Owen, you also might think that was amazing. And on Sundays he takes the bins out and has even been known to load the dishwasher – badly but at least he tries. How about you, Janice?"

"Friday. It's got to be Fridays. I stop work at eleven and the rest of the day is mine."

Martha returned the querying. "Really? Nothing special other than not working. How about Saturday and Sunday – you don't work on those days."

"No it's Fridays. Straight after work I wander off into town and go to a swank hotel for an elegant cup of tea. Then perhaps do some window shopping in the jewellery stores or decide which clothes to purchase to make Lucie in accounts dead jealous. It's basically quiet uneventful me time before heading home to Jaxon and the kids."

"You do that every Friday? No wonder Lucie refers to you as a walking wardrobe."

When 11 o'clock came that Friday, Janice waved goodbye to Martha. "See you Monday."

Martha smiled back. "Yeh – go have your relaxing me time. You've earned it this week what with the company audit."

Janice chose the Sheraton Hotel for her weekly up-market late morning tea. It came with an assortment of biscuits – chocolate ones, almond covered delicacies and caramel coated shortbread. Once all had been consumed, she paid with her contactless card – this dining room was too up-market for dirty cash.

And then as she walked through the lobby, her world changed. Her pleasant quiet was replaced by abject fear and heart pounding. A man had grabbed her arm, twisted it violently behind her back as he whispered in her ear. "Don't yell or I'll break your arm. Just act normally and nothing bad will happen."

In a soft voice so as to do as she'd been told and not raise alarm, she whispered. "You're hurting me. What have I done? Why me? Whatever you think it is you've got the wrong person."

He growled back in her ear as he began frog marching her towards the lifts. "I know what I'm doing so just walk normally." To make sure she understood, he pulled her arm up slightly – the one he'd forced behind her back. She took in a sharp breath with a muffled ouch.

In the lift he pressed 7 which sent her mind racing. Seven? I thought he'd be taking me downstairs to the parking lot. Oh God, what's happening?

She knew that above the fourth floor it was just rooms, some suites but no public spaces. And at this hour probably no house staff she could alert.

"Doors Opening – Seventh Floor." Words which caused Janice to begin to shake with fear – the time for just trembling having long passed. She thought he must already have a room here. Should she shout and holler for help. Not much point – most of the rooms at this hour would be empty and he said he'd break my arm if I made a sound.

Room 723. With his free hand he swiped the electronic lock and the door swung open. The room was empty. Well it was empty until he shoved her in, closed the door behind them and twisted the lock.

With one quick flick of his hand he hurled her on to the bed and before she could even respond, he was on top of her holding her head down painfully with a handful of her hair while the other hand started groping, fondling and beginning to undress her.

Janice had read enough detective and crime stories to know that struggling against this sex driven maniac could easily inflame him to the point her life could be in danger so she just acquiesced to his advances and actions. As she attempted to relax she forced her mind to think of after. What would happen after this man was finished.

It didn't take long before he got up from the bed, rearranged his clothes and headed for the door. She felt at least her life had been spared. Changed maybe but at least spared. Could she even tell Jaxon what happened?

At the door he turned and snarled. "Don't even think of telling anyone – remember I know where you live."

With those sharp words, he opened the door and sauntered out as if nothing had happened leaving Janice shaking and fighting for breath in short intakes. Again she was thankful that at least he hadn't killed her.

Just then the door opened again and the brute stuck his head back into the room. "Same time next week Janice? I suggest we use the Hilton – we haven't been there for a while."

"Yeah sure. See you Monday, Aiden."

NEVER GIVE UP

As the sun began setting over the jungle canopy, the siren sounded to call the men back to the camp. The day had been blisteringly hot and the men were exhausted beyond belief. But this was just like every other day. These Allied prisoners of war captured by the Japanese were being used as slaves to build the Burma railway.

There was a major cultural difference between the prisoners and their captors. In the Japanese minds, a soldier would never surrender – he would fight until killed. To surrender was the greatest dishonour imaginable and those who would do so were to be regarded as the lowest form of life – not even human. Because the Allied soldiers had surrendered rather than fight to the death, they were treated as disposable scum with absolutely no respect shown to them, not even for their lives.

As the men trudged back to the camp, some were assigned the most unpleasant task – that of bringing back the bodies of those who had died that day while working. Died from exhaustion, malnutrition, disease – or all three. To the Japanese, the death of a POW was a mixed blessing – one less mouth to feed but also one less slave worker.

After a disgusting bowl of putrid rice, the imprisoned Allied officers gathered to discuss the day and ascertain the day's tally.

"How many died today?"

"At work or in the hospital?"

"Both."

"Only two in the field today but three in the hospital – dysentery and septic shock."

One officer spoke up, "Four men in my company are planning to escape. Their aim is to go back down the line and sabotage some of the railway."

"They do know what will happen if they are caught, don't they? Summary execution in front of the camp."

"Yes. They said they were going to die anyway so at least this way they would be dying doing something positive rather than just succumbing to disease."

The senior officer spoke. "I'm not sure. You know the Japanese have promised extreme retribution if anyone even tries to escape. They will be even harsher if the men are caught damaging the rail line."

"Are you forbidding it?"

"Officially yes. Unofficially I'm not condoning it but I admire their bravery. But equally, I fear the consequences – greater starvation, reduced medicine, as if that was even possible, and perhaps immediate murder of all hospital patients."

"You're right. I'll tell them not to escape. As you say, it could have disastrous consequences for the rest of us."

The four men were told not to escape but although they listened, they agreed amongst themselves to defy this order. They couldn't just wait to die of starvation or disease. During the night, armed with various tools, they crept out without being seen.

In some camps, there was a thrice daily roll call. Not however in this camp. The jungle surrounding the camp was so impenetrable and dangerous, the Japanese felt nobody would be stupid enough to try and escape. Since the work force was being depleted each day anyway through death and sickness, the disappearance of the four went unnoticed.

However, a few days later the recall siren sounded in the middle of the morning. Everyone knew this meant trouble and returned with a great sense of foreboding. At the camp they were herded together so they could all see the four escaped prisoners who had been caught. Then in the sight of all inmates, the four were forced to kneel on the ground and were shot in the head. On pain of instant death, the prisoners were told to leave the bodies rotting in the sun as a constant reminder not to escape.

As if this was not enough general punishment, four officers selected at random were hauled away and placed in the 'ovens'. These were tiny corrugated iron huts placed so that the blazing sun would heat them to intolerable temperatures. Before being put in these 'ovens', the officers were forced to remove their trouser belts. This was done to prevent them committing suicide in the ovens.

The men were then sent back to work.

When the siren sounded again at the end of the day and the prisoners returned, they saw the four officers standing in the main square facing four firing squads. The officers stood in a row without shirts on and with their arms around their stomachs to hold up their trousers.

The camp commandant appeared and had enough English to enable him to make his speech without an interpreter.

"You not good ocifers. I say no escape. You let four men escape. You not worthy be ocifers. You no control you men. You have no honour. I no need you. You not real men. Other ocifers learn. They not obey me, they also die. You not honourable men – you die now."

He paused. "Raise you arms above head."

The four officers did as they were told and put their arms in the air which meant their trousers fell down around their ankles. Because of the heat they wore no underwear so they now stood basically naked. They knew their fate was sealed. Nothing could be done now to save them.

But before the commandant could give the order to fire, one officer, call him Major Jameson, put his hand out and waved it back and forth while he stooped down and pulled his trousers back up with the other hand. He then wrapped his arms around his stomach to hold up his trousers and with a stern look stood facing the camp commandant.

The camp commandant repeated his order, "Raise you arms above head."

Major Jameson did as he was told and his trousers fell down again. So he repeated his previous actions, waving to stop the shooting while he pulled up his trousers again and then wrapped his arms around his stomach to hold his trousers up. He was determined he would not be shot naked with his trousers around his ankles.

The commandant looked directly at Major Jameson and shouted his order, "Raise you arms above head."

Major Jameson repeated the whole rigmarole – arms up, trousers fall down, wave to stop proceedings, pull up trousers and stand tall with arms around stomach to hold trousers up yet again.

There was a long silence broken finally when the commandant spoke in Japanese to one of his aides. The aide went over to Major Jameson and in halting English said, "You come."

Major Jameson still with his arms around his waist to keep his trousers up was escorted to stand directly in front of the commandant. The two men looked directly at each other for what felt like an eternity. There was total silence around the square. No one could even surmise what would happen next. Would the commandant strike Major Jameson down; would he beat him; would he do the execution himself using his own pistol? All of these seemed equally likely outcomes.

After a long silent eye to eye confrontation, the commandant spoke. "Mayor Yimsin. Why you do that?"

In a totally calm voice the major replied. "It is not honourable for an officer to be shot in front of his men with his trousers down."

The silence continued, broken finally by the commandant. "I see you courageous man. You also honourable man. You no die."

And in one of the most surreal moments of his life that stayed forever in Major Jameson's memory, the Japanese commandant bowed to the Major and the Major bowed back.

Although the other three officers were then executed without further delay, Major Jameson's actions gave all the watching men the courage to have hope and realize the importance of never giving up.

Major Jameson survived the camp, survived the war and remained in the armed forces.

Author's Note

When I lived in Canada, the event depicted in this story was told to me in my parents' house by a Canadian military doctor who witnessed this extraordinary exchange while a Prisoner Of War in Burma. Obviously the name has been changed but the doctor did confirm to us that the officer in question did survive the war - by having the presence of mind to never give up and by refusing to be executed with his trousers down.

JEROME'S FINGER

The phone rang in Dax's house. "Hello?"

"Hi. It's Jerome here. You remember me? Jerome Taylor."

There was a gasp at the other end, "You can't be. I shot Jerome five years ago! What the hell's this? A sick joke?"

"No Dax. You *thought* you killed me five years ago."

"But I buried you myself."

"You buried someone. But it wasn't me. D'you remember the explosion? The fire?"

"How could I forget? I only just got your body out before the fuzz arrived."

"Not my body! So. Tell me why – why d'you do it?"

"I thought you were double crossin' me — become a canary. So I had no choice – I had to shoot you an' I couldn't leave your body there – it would tie me to that job an' I wasn't goin' down for that job. No way, not never … and if it wasn't you I buried, then who the hell was it?"

"Hey. Don't ask me – I wasn't there, remember? I don't know who you shot and buried."

"I'm not likin' this and you sound slightly different. How do I know you're really Jerome?"

The caller was prepared and uttered just six words. "The hidden well – 27 Chester Street."

Another gasp. "Ok. Only you an' I knew about that well and what we put down inside it. Good God. Perhaps it is you. Where've you been and what the hell you callin' up now for?"

"Stop askin' questions Dax and listen. Where I've been, trust me, you don't wanna know – and as to why I'm callin' – simple – my share of the ten million."

"It's mostly gone. There's not much left now."

"So that means all that's left is mine. And I want it now."

"It'll take time."

"It won't take time for me to repay you for tryin' to take me out. Only, unlike you — I will get it right, so it'll be bye bye Dax unless you act now. Not tomorrow. Now!"

"Yeh, you? Get rid of me? Who you kiddin'?"

"Dax, I know where you live. I know where your kids go to school."

"Tryin' to frighten me? Try harder."

"Ok. Look out the window. See the man there lookin' up at you? He's one of mine. Wave at him with your left hand."

Dax was right handed and instinctively waved that hand.

There was silence for a moment and then the unnerving conversation resumed.

"Dax — I said LEFT HAND. D'you believe me now?"

Dax pulled back from the window and began to shake. If Jerome was really alive he might seek more than just his share.

"You're being quiet Dax. I don't like that."

"I still don't believe it's you, Jerome. The Jerome I knew wouldn't threaten my kids."

"Rich, comin' from a guy who thought he'd murdered me. The Jerome you knew has changed. As you've just seen – I've got a little group now."

"Yeh? So what? I still don't believe it's you."

"You don't believe it's me? Stupid risk, Dax. If you love your kids and want to see them again, you'll go an' check."

"Check what?"

"Remember, I'm missing the little finger on me left hand? The one that Mad Boy Cullen axed off. Well since you don't believe it's me talkin', check the fingers on the guy you buried and you'll find no fingers missin'. Get my point? But don't do anythin' stupid. Remember – your kids will be comin' out of school soon. And I want my share. I'll call back once you've had a chance to check the body."

The phone call ended.

Soon after, Dax was seen putting a shovel in his car and driving off.

Back at the station the Inspector congratulated the Cold Case Team. "I think it worked. The garden well bit was a guess but from the video feed, Dax looked rattled as he left the house. We should be able to follow him with the three tracers planted on his car and if he digs up the body we can arrest him for Jerome's murder. And Phoebe, well done. I had my doubts about that voice synthesizer you mentioned. How did you do it? How did you get my voice to sound like Jerome?"

"I used some new software, sir, that changes a voice to sound like someone else's voice. You supply the program with some samples of the chosen voice and it changes what you say to sound like that other person."

The Inspector looked puzzled. "But Jerome disappeared five years ago."

Phoebe smiled. "You're right, sir, but we still had the interview tapes from when he was questioned about Chester Street – just before he disappeared."

"Nice work team! Now, let's go get him."

MY GREATEST ACHIEVEMENT

People and dogs and training. I'm normally patient but it was becoming exasperating. Every day the same – no change – no improvement. It was as if she just did not want to learn.

I'm not one for books. I can't understand them. Anyway, what do authors really know about my circumstance? They speculate – they pontificate – they try to say everything can be taught through reward or punishment. What's the phrase – *carrot or stick*?

Stupid. Who wants a carrot? Maybe a donkey? And who wants a stick? What are you supposed to do with a stick? You can hardly use it to threaten unless the object of your threat understands the implication of you brandishing a stick. Heaven knows I've tried and all I get back is a sort of smile.

We've gone out for walks. She's always attached on a lead as if she might get lost. I mean really. She should know by now how to get home without me. And then there's the occasions she meets up with others. They just stand around – sometimes putting their faces together. At times like that I've tried pulling on the lead but that hardly ever works – she's too big and strong.

Finally, a few weeks ago she noticed the thing about playing with a ball. But in the beginning that was a disaster. The ball would be thrown far away and after a short wait I'd have to go and get it back – she just wouldn't learn. It took a long time for her to understand the concept of a reward – balls and biscuits going together. Once she understood that, life became much more tolerable. A short throw, the ball is brought back and then there's a biscuit. A short throw and a biscuit. It's been that way for days now.

Getting that into her brain is what I regard as one of my major achievements. The next objective is to change the brand of biscuits. I hate these dog biscuits she keeps giving me – I much prefer the custard creams she has with tea when we get home and I sit on her lap.

HOUSE SITTING

It was late on Tuesday afternoon when Steve walked over to Danny's desk.

"Dan, you got time for a drink before going home?"

"Sure. Not got much else to do after I finish this report. See you outside at five?"

And so it was at just after five, the two friends wandered down the road to the local pub for a quick pint. This pub was known for its broad range of artisan ales and they both decided to try the new one with the enticing name *'Never Again'*. The publican refused to enlighten them as to whether *never again* referred to drinking another pint of this brew, or never again drinking something else. They'd have to form their own opinion.

After a most satisfying sip and gulp, they both agreed it was certainly a passable brew and might even merit a repeat if they found their glasses were empty. But they did not let such considerations stop them from chatting and sharing the latest gossip – which included rumours about themselves.

"Dan – I've heard on the grapevine that Sharon and you have parted ways. Is that right?"

"If by *parting ways* you mean me throwing her out of the house and my life, then you've heard rightly. It wasn't so much what she was doing – as what she was not doing."

Steve tipped his head to one side as he smiled a conspiratorial smirk. "Oh so she was refusing to —"

Dan interrupted before Steve could say anything more. "No – Steve. Far from it. What she was not doing was adhering to any concept of commitment. I found out her late nights in her office did not entail what one might call work – she was playing me for a fool so – schoop – I kicked her out and I'm glad I did."

"Is that why you said you hadn't much else to do after work? No one else taking Sharon's place?"

"Hey – give a man a break – she only left or should I say was kicked out on Sunday – so no, there's no one even on the horizon."

"That's good and potentially makes it easier for you."

"Easier? What are you getting at?"

"Well, you see I have to visit our client in Singapore later this week and all of next and I was wondering if you'd be willing to house sit for me – all perks included."

Knowing that Steve's house had an 85 inch TV with cinema sound, a sauna on the ground floor and a Jacuzzi and barbecue on the patio, Dan did not find it hard to accept the invitation.

However, Steve threw a curve ball into the plan when he warned Dan about certain aspects of the place. "I hope you're not allergic to cats."

"No – I like cats. So is there a cat there? I didn't know you had a cat?"

Steve nodded. "You could say that, but I'm sure you'll get along fine – a bit of feeding – a bit of cuddling – you know the kind of stuff. There's an electronic door so you shouldn't have to worry about strays. I'm sure I don't need to leave instructions. It's one of the reasons I can't just lock the house up. So are you on for this, starting Thursday?"

Dan nodded agreement and Steve handed him a spare key. "By the way – the alarm is under the stairs and you should be able to remember the number – it's my extension."

After work on Thursday, Steve left for his Qantas flight and Dan drove to the house.

Although there was no sign of the furry feline, Steve had left ten cans of cat food on the countertop and Dan spied an empty bowl on the floor. Not knowing how much to put out, Dan emptied half a can into the bowl and put it carefully back on the floor. As for the cans, he arranged them neatly in a square pattern on the counter top – three by three – Dan liked things to be neat and orderly.

That evening he felt he was part of the playing team as he watched premier football on the wide screen. He stayed up so late, he had no time to sample the Jacuzzi or the sauna. As he crawled into the super king-sized bed he promised himself that those other perks would be tried over the weekend.

Friday morning – a quick splash in the enormous walk-in shower – two slices of toast and coffee in the kitchen and then off to work. However, when he returned back that evening, he was puzzled. He was sure he'd left the cans in a square but now they were all in a single neat row. He decided he must have been wrong as cans cannot move on their own.

He realized too late that he had failed to bring any food for himself. He noticed the bowl on the floor was not yet empty so there was no need to worry about feeding the cat. Since it was too late to start cooking, he decided to head out for a meal at a local restaurant which was only a short walk down the road. And that was a good thing because the restaurant had excellent wine and brandies and by the time Dan returned he could not have driven. He needed more caffeine so he went into the kitchen for a quick brew but stopped short at the door and began wondering if he was losing his mind – the cans of food were now in two rows.

As he crawled again back into the oversized bed, having watched a cinema sized film on the oversized TV, he spoke to himself. "Tomorrow I'll buy me a steak with all the trimmings and use Steve's barbecue and wallow in the Jacuzzi with my meal on one of the floating trays Steve has out there."

The bed was so comfortable, Dan slept until mid morning. But he did not dally – out he went to purchase his forthcoming feast. His car was well laden down with comestibles of the most extravagant nature – Dan was not going to waste this opportunity to live in luxury.

But – and this was a major but – he was not prepared for what he found when he returned to the house and opened the door – there was a smell of cooking wafting enticingly from the kitchen along with a voice which called out, "I was not expecting you back – did they cancel the trip?"

Dan felt he needed to investigate so he carefully tiptoed to the kitchen whereupon he saw the source of the voice was a very attractive young lady busy stirring a large pot of what appeared to be chilli.

Since he knew he was the official house sitter he felt he had the right to enquire as to what this image of pulchritude was doing in the house. "Excuse me but who are you?"

She turned around so quickly she forgot to put the large wooden spoon down and was able without any effort to cover him in a splat of hot red sauce. "Sorry about that – but I might ask the same – who are you and what are you doing here?"

"Although I asked first, I'll provide my reason – I work with Steve and he asked me to house sit while he's in Singapore. And your reason please – you appear to be accustomed to being in this kitchen?"

As she started to speak, the lady wiped her hands on the blue and white tiny apron which failed to hide her elegant figure. "Steve's my brother and since my boyfriend left me a few weeks ago, Steve said I could come here any time I wanted. It appears he must have forgotten that in spite of asking you, he also asked me to house sit this week. Oh – this could become awkward."

However, after eyeing Dan's gym toned frame for a moment – a rather long moment – she spoke again. "Well since you're here, do you like chilli – it would be a waste to throw it out."

For the second time that week, Dan felt it was only sensible to agree to an unexpected offer. "That sounds like a great idea. I have some red wine in these bags or would you prefer beer?"

"Beer goes with this strength of chilli, so yes beer it will be."

Dan realized he might be able to solve a rather perplexing conundrum. "Can I ask – was it you who rearranged the cans of cat food Steve put on the counter?"

"Yes, but I don't know why they are even here. As far as I know Steve doesn't have a cat."

"Funny – I'm sure when Steve asked me to house sit he mentioned a cat and said I should look after a cat."

"I'll have to have words with my brother when he returns. By the way I have already turned on the Jacuzzi so shall we eat this meal in there on the floating trays? It's a rather special Jacuzzi – it has waterproof speakers so we can eat to the sound of slow jazz – if that's acceptable?"

Dan was wondering if he was still having a dream until he noticed his chilli splattered clothes and knew he would not have included that in his dream so this must be reality – a rather odd reality – so he concurred with her suggestion. "Sure – that sounds good. Perhaps I should introduce myself – I'm Dan."

"Hi Dan – I figured it was you. My brother speaks often about you and his description of you was fairly accurate."

Dan was slightly taken aback by this comment – but only slightly. "If Steve is your brother, then may I assume you are Susan – the sister he keeps idolizing?"

"Yes I'm Susan ——— but Steve always calls me Cat."

GOING SOMEWHERE ARE WE?

Andrew stood on the side of the sea loch looking wistfully out at the raging onslaught of waves. He'd seldom seen such waves. Higher than a man of medium build. Crashing on the shore with the roar of an angry lion. And then coursing back out to sea dragging with it anything moveable in the rush to meet the next tower of cascading water.

He stood transfixed for more than an hour hoping for some reduction in the tumultuous sea but knowing from experience such hope was doomed to be dashed by the over-bearing incessant inclement weather.

He had a job to complete. He'd been paid by the man who now sat in Andrew's cubby hole – good coins that rattled in his sporran as the wind swirled around his kilt. The cubby hole was more a cave than a building though over time he'd added some sheltering walls partially built of drift wood and partially patched together with moss and peat. Normally he used this hovel for contraband and other items the locals considered as essentials but which the dastardly Sassenach revenue collectors wished to tax or perhaps impound – most likely for their own private benefit and use.

But tonight, the cubby hole was home to a strange man – a man of noble deportment as Andrew had easily ascertained from his vestments. Mere peasant mortals never sport feathers in their flowing hats nor sashes round their body as this fine gentleman did. And he had paid Andrew to help him – good coins they were, some of silver, some of gold.

Help he'd asked for. And help Andrew was giving him by currently keeping his visitor hidden from seeking eyes. When the man stated he wished to cross to the far island, Andrew had retorted he'd come to the right man as he also wished to go to that very same place, though Andrew was sure, but did not voice, doubtless for a different purpose.

He'd not enquired why such a richly attired person would be asking to be taken hence by such a shifty looking scallywag as Andrew knew he appeared — those coins he'd been paid rendered the asking of such questions inappropriate. He surmised perhaps they both shared an intense desire to remain virtually invisible. Andrew, in order to accomplish his smuggling whilst retaining his freedom and this man, who for whatever withheld reason felt it was worth a few gold coins to remain unseen and hidden.

But the weather continued its relentless display of force. Daylight would soon be upon these two, Andrew and the unknown man, thus rendering the intended transportation assistance impossible. Even if the loch were to be as flat as a cooking stone, Andrew could not take the man to the island during the day for fear of being seen by the revenue collectors – his burly frame was well known to those who sought to imprison him. And he thought perhaps the same it might be for his erstwhile companion.

In consideration of the impending sunrise, Andrew feared if he could not ferry this unknown fellow to yon far island, might the much valued coins be at risk? But then, upon further reflection, he reasoned to himself he might be able to render a different favour and thereby retain his bounty.

"Ah canny tak ye across de wa'er noo the day is here, but my sister's friend's husband's cousin's brother-in-law's daughter might be able to render ye mair help than I at dis time o' day. 'Er name be Flora, an' I can bu' ask 'er if ye want. Who shall I say be needin' 'elp?"

The noble man looked pained and distressed at this news but replied. "Oh well be that as it may. You can tell your sister's friend's husband's cousin's brother-in-law's daughter, that Charles, sometimes known as Bonnie Prince Charlie, be willing to don the clothing and appearance of a servile maid be this daughter willing to take him, thus disguised, to Skye."

And so Andrew did as bid and upon his return with good news, the man gave him another coin for his troubles and set off to meet this Flora MacDonald, to be taken across the sea to Skye.

STUCK IN KUALA LUMPUR

It was Wednesday and my bags were packed. Unfortunately, on Monday I had received word that my contract was not being renewed and my interview for a job in another part of the company had not been successful. It was time to go home back to England.

Outside, the mid-day heat was unbearable but at least in the Holiday Inn the oppressive Kuala Lumpur summer sun and high humidity was countered by the overly effective air conditioning – swelter to shiver through a rotating door.

At reception I smiled at the girl behind the counter. I'd been here long enough the staff felt like family. "Rani, can you get me a taxi to the airport, please."

I hoped the taxi would have Air Conditioning but often they just had open windows.

"Certainly Mr Fred. I think there's one outside right now. Bola! Take Mr Fred's cases to taxi car. You be staying with us again, hopefully, yes?"

"I doubt it Rani. I didn't get the job so I'm off home. Please tell Sharifa and the others goodbye and thanks from me."

My heart sank as I stepped into the car. This was an open window taxi with seats that had been sat on and worn to the point they hardly qualified as seats – they were now merely a tangle of entrapped springs. And the driver was a talker.

"Going home, sah."

"Yes back to London."

"London. Very big. I watch game when can. You like Manchester United, yes?"

"That's not a London team."

"Oh sorry, sah. Chelsea. Yes. You support Chelsea, yes?"

"Actually, I don't watch football."

My answer obviously caused extreme consternation and confusion for the driver and he stopped conversing. An English person who does not watch football? Does not compute.

The blissful silence lasted for quite a while only to be replaced by a deafening honking of car horns. We were now stuck in one of KL's infamous traffic jams. They had been known to last for hours as no one would surrender an inch. Instead the drivers just attempted to disperse the obstructing vehicles through a barrage of sound by leaning on the horn.

"Is there another way around?"

"You have plane to catch?"

"Yes that's why I'm going to the airport. Is there another way past these cars?"

"Oh no, sah. We stay here and maybe traffic move."

"But I'll miss my plane."

"You go London? What plane?"

"Qantas."

"Oh sorry, sah. Today, you no miss plane – plane miss you."

"What d'you mean?"

"I check flight times and we not make Qantas flight today. Too big traffic. We stuck here and no get Subang in time. Maybe tomorrow, sah."

"Tomorrow? Oh Great."

"You want we go airport and you sleep on benches or back to hotel? Airport have nice benches."

"Back to the hotel, please."

"I turn left here and go this road and get back fastly, sah."

"Why did you not go this way to the airport?"

"I always go on main road to airport."

"But you get stuck in traffic on the main road."

"Yes, sah, you right. We many times get stuck. But scenery nicer on main road."

I sat back and fell silent. I assumed there was some logic to what he said but I was too tired to enter into such a discussion. However, I did risk a continuation of our discourse when I noticed in his race to get back to the hotel he always slowed down at green lights, but drove quite nonchalantly through red ones. When I asked for an explanation of this odd behaviour, he answered. "Oh sah. I go slow on green – so many bad drivers go through on red."

When we arrived back at the hotel, Rani was still in reception. "Ah Mr Fred. You not away long. You come back to us so soon, yes?"

"Yes, a room for the night please, Rani."

After some rapid clicking on the booking machine she looked up. "Ah your favourite room. Bola! Take Mr Fred's cases his normal room. Oh I almost forget. Message come for you just after you left. Here."

And Rani passed me a slip of paper. When I opened it up, I almost ran out to thank the taxi driver for his illogically slow and unsuccessful attempt to reach the airport. The message read.

> *My secretary mis-read my writing. I had scribbled a quick note on your CV. She thought I wrote* **'job – no'**. *What I wrote was* **'job – now'**. *If you still want the job, let me know by Thursday.*

"Rani, can you pass me a phone please? It looks as if I'll be staying for a while."

Author's Note

While working in Kuala Lumpur for a few months, I stayed at the Holiday Inn. The traffic experience portrayed in the story is based on a genuine conversation with one of the taxi drivers.

WRITER'S GROUNDHOG

Sasa muttered with annoyance, "Yes, yes, YES —— that's why I pressed DELETE – so just do it!"

Sasa's frustration and anger was often aimed at her laptop. Especially when her mind went blank or could only keep writing out the same idea over and over and over again.

Although she recognised that computers were great when it came to rewriting, she felt they lacked that sense of physical interaction.

She thought back to the earlier days. The days of pencil and paper. There was something cathartic about ripping the paper off the pad, scrunching it up into a ball and aiming it at the basket. And then came the throw – if she could hit that smudge on the wall where the spider had met its end then the paper ball would bounce back and land in the bin.

She never fully understood if she kept missing the bin because of bad aim or as a subconscious excuse to use up even more time. If she missed, she could not just get up and put the ball in the basket – oh no – she had to sit back down and try the throw again. But computers have a DELETE button —— no opportunity for delay tactics.

She began to wonder if she was suffering from writer's block – that tendency to keep starting all over again with the same words. She was concerned she might be in a loop.

No – No I just need coffee. Definitely time for coffee – my mind will be refreshed by a cup. In the kitchen she pondered slowly – would I think better after Costa Rican coffee or Columbian? Or perhaps I should go to the shop and get that new Indonesian blend? To help with this major time consuming decision, she stood at the window staring at the bird feeder.

Oh, I must replenish the bird feeder. She knew it was only yesterday that she had somehow found time to top it up but perhaps it should be done again – maybe a flock of hungry robins might come by. It was irrelevant that she had never seen a flock of robins – but you never know – so the feeder needed topping up.

The bird food was kept in the small cupboard above the sink. *Goodness me – when did I last clean this sink – it looks filthy.* Rubber gloves, bleach, scrubbing brush – out they came from wherever she had hidden them and soon the sink was gleaming.

Now what was I doing? Something in the garden – oh yes – the roses need pruning. Sasa then made that fully understandable rationalization – writing can be done at night but not rose pruning. She was not avoiding facing that blank page – she was exercising time management.

But were there enough gardening bags for all the rose prunings she might produce? Perhaps a trip to the shop for more bags? After all it would be imprudent to begin pruning without having sufficient bags.

I could take the car but they say a walk helps clear the mind. Sasa had not fully taken account of the fact her mind was currently quite clear – clear of any thoughts or ideas at all – in fact as blank as that dreaded empty laptop screen with its silly winking cursor.

Boots, hat, coat, or perhaps the other coat? But that means the green hat which is upstairs. In a crowning moment of concentration Sasa got the green hat without being distracted. And so she set off to the shops. Down the road or through the woods on that nice new path? After much consideration, the path won out.

As Sasa strolled along she heard the birds making mating calls in response to the squeaking of her boots. The path went through an old cemetery and Sasa stopped to read some of the stones. Many were partially covered with moss and lichen but in the corner was one that attracted her attention. From a distance she could not decide if it had fallen over or had been laid flat as some sort of lid or weight.

She scraped back the moss and read the inscription – she had never seen anything like it.

> Here lieth the rotting remains of
> Frederick Fitzgerald
> Tax collector until dead 15 October 1752
> Despised brother of Jonathan
> Loathed son of his evil parents
> Mildred and Samuel Fitzgerald
> "May his soul forever cycle around beneath this block"

She read it once — she read it twice. And then with no one looking she danced a merry jig around the stone. A story had come to her mind. The words in the stone had brought forth a tale and she knew she had a story to tell. Two words was all it took – *cycle* and *block*.

With a rapid change of plan, she skipped on home. Gone was the shopping spree for plastic bags – gone was the distraction of pruning roses or filling up the bird feeder. Not even the thought of coffee could stand in her way. Gone too was her writer's block.

With renewed vigour Sasa began typing furiously on the laptop keyboard. Without hesitation she hammered away. She always began with the title of the piece as it helped focus her mind.

Thereafter the words flowed – *as if she had seen them before.*

Writer's Groundhog

Sasa muttered with annoyance, "Yes, yes, YES —— that's why I pressed DELETE – so just do it!"

Sasa's frustration and anger was often aimed at her laptop. Especially when her mind went blank or could only keep thinking of and writing out the same idea over and over and over again.

Although she recognised that computers were great when it came to rewriting, she felt they lacked that sense of physical interaction.

She thought back to the earlier days. The days of pencil and paper. There was something cathartic about ripping the paper off the pad, scrunching it up into a ball and aiming it at the basket. And then came the throw – if she could hit that smudge on the wall where the spider had met its end then the paper ball would bounce back and land in the bin.

She never fully understood if she kept missing the bin because of bad aim or as a subconscious excuse to use up even more time. If she missed, she could not just get up and put the ball in the basket – oh no – she had to sit back down and try the throw again. But computers have a DELETE button —— no opportunity for delay tactics.

She began to wonder if she was suffering from writer's block – that tendency to keep starting all over again with the same ——

At this point Adriana stopped typing, took a sip of her now lukewarm coffee, moved the cursor to the top of her laptop screen and clicked on the little circular arrow.

Instantly a message appeared on her screen which said ——

TO CONTINUE GO TO PARAGRAPH 6 ON PAGE 110

IN A CRISIS

My outstanding ability to cope in a crisis is exemplified by the traumatic situation I experienced in my early years in which after breaking the lead in my HB pencil, I looked around the room and saw that Eloisha Stanson MacDonald, the little girl in the corner, had a very large pencil whereupon I sauntered over and asked politely in a gentle voice if I could share it with her but when the young toddler looked up with a sour face, pulled her tongue out and said no, I grabbed the pencil, broke it in two and gave the impudent little devil the smaller half whereupon the child changed her demeanour, smiled and clapped a loud thank you which pleased me so much that I repeated the action, breaking her smaller half yet again but this was not so successful as the ensuing wailing and gnashing of teeth that was induced by the bruising, contusion and bleeding gash caused when that bad tempered little monster kicked me in the shins was so alarming that it was felt necessary to call for an ambulance to provide professional medical care and attention which resulted in me being told that I needed to be taken to the hospital for stitches which meant, in fact, that I no longer needed a pencil to draw a picture of a dragon.

For some reason, I never really liked pre-school.

Author's Note

This was written as part of a creative writing class exercise in which we were asked to write one long continuous flow sentence. The first paragraph / sentence is 225 words long.

AMERICANO

Part 1

When Helen and Gail came into the university cafe carrying some books and papers, it was fairly full of people chatting away. The two of them continued their animated conversation and sat down at an empty table which had four chairs.

Helen was talking. "And then Tom hit her."

Her friend expressed astonishment. "What? You mean punched her like?"

"I think so. But it was all so fast it was difficult to tell. Sadie seemed to fall but caught the edge of the table with her hand."

"Was she hurt?"

"More stunned than hurt. But she was really annoyed. Furious you could say."

"I don't understand why Tom would do that – punching Sadie."

"Well you know he does have a short temper and Sadie had just called him a lazy good for nothing slob and didn't want anything more to do with him."

As they were talking, a waiter kept going back and forth clearing up dirty dishes and taking orders to other customers. He did not come over to take their order.

Gail asked Helen a question. "Is Sadie seeing someone else?"

"No. But Tom thinks she is. But then Tom's a liar. Cheats on her every week with Nancy."

"What? Tom's two timing Sadie?"

With disgust Helen expressed her opinion about Tom's actions. "I'd hate to be going out with someone so deceitful and nasty."

"Me to. Fortunately Adam's not like that."

The waiter finally came to their table and asked. "You two look tired from all that studying. Can I get you something? What would you like? Your usual?"

Gail responded. "Not yet thanks, We're waiting for Adam and Bert."

Helen looked at her watch. "Guess what. The boys are late. But we'll wait for them. Ok?"

The waiter nodded. "Yeh, sure, just call me over when you're ready." He resumed walking back and forth delivering drinks and clearing up.

Helen picked up the conversation again. "Seeing Sadie thumped like that was very dramatic and rather frightening."

"Were the police called? I mean if he was hitting her, that's surely assault? No?"

"I don't know – it ended there. They didn't show a trailer for the next episode so we'll have to wait 'til next Tuesday to find out."

"Does Bert watch it with you?"

Helen looked slightly surprised. "Oh no. He can't stand soaps. Also, after the show I get on with my studying. That engineering option's a hard course. No, he goes out with the boys. We don't see each other on Tuesdays." And then after a pause she continued. "Or Thursdays and sometimes Saturdays either coming to think of it."

"Is he seeing someone else?"

"What? My Bert? Good heavens no. He says he only has eyes for me and I'm sure it's true. If he was like Tom – seeing other girls – I'd dump him immediately. But No. No. We agreed – we'd only see each other. We agreed that at the beginning of term."

"Lucky you."

"Come on, Gail. The way you two act I thought you and Adam were knitted together."

"Adam's great, yes, and I know we agreed to see only each other but I'm not sure if he'd even notice if I went out with someone else."

"I'm sure he would if you actually went out. But if someone asked you out, would you go?"

"No. Of course not."

"But what if someone asked you out in front of Adam. D'you think he'd react?"

Gail responded with a smile. "Hopefully so, but that's not likely to happen, is it?"

"It could be arranged. It'd be interesting to see what he did."

Gail seemed slightly puzzled. "Maybe, but why would I do that?"

"It'd tell you how he actually felt about you."

"I suppose. But what did you mean *it could be arranged*?"

"We could get someone to pretend to ask you out when Adam was there."

"What? Even if I wanted to do this, where would we find someone willing to do that? Especially since I'd be turning him down."

"Yeh, of course you'd turn down the invite – but only after seeing how Adam reacted. Come on, Gail. It could be fun."

"Fun for us maybe, but how about the guy? He'd have to come here, pretend to invite me out, stand there as I turned him down and then go away. That'd be cruel. Nice idea, but no way. You're not going to find anyone to do that."

"I think I can. I already have someone in mind."

"What? You're serious about this, aren't you?"

"Absolutely. If I had any doubts about Bert, I'd want to know how he felt."

"But I don't have any doubts about Adam. Do you doubt Bert?"

"Not at all – he's great and I trust him completely."

"As I said – lucky you."

"But we're not talking about me – we're talking about you and Adam. Anyway, what do you mean – lucky me?"

"Because Bert shows his affection for you. I just never quite know with Adam. He's so quiet I wonder at times if he even knows I'm there."

"That's why we want to wake him up. Get him to realize he needs to show how he feels. So are you on for this?"

"Maybe – it depends. You said someone in mind. Who? Do I know him already?"

"Yep. In fact, he's here right now."

"What? Where?"

Gail looked around but failed to see anyone suitable. "I don't see anyone."

"William!"

Gail was puzzled. "William? Who's William?"

"William – the waiter."

"Him? You cannot be serious."

"Oh but I am. He'd be perfect and I'm sure he'd be willing."

And before Gail could object, Helen called him over. "William! Can you come here a moment?"

"Be right there." William took the dirty plates he was carrying away and came to their table.

"Ok girls, decided what you want? Your usual? A Cappuccino and a Latte? Is that right?"

Helen spoke. "Nothing right now. But we have a small favour to ask."

"A favour? Of course – you're regulars here so how can I help?"

Helen looked at William with a questioning expression and spoke. "This may seem odd but we want you to pretend to ask Gail out on a date."

"Odd? I think I'd use the word weird. Why would I do that? Let alone why would I pretend to do that?"

Gail reassured him. "Oh I'll be refusing, so you don't need to worry."

"Oh I wasn't worrying. But if I'm pretending to invite you out will you be just pretending to refuse?"

"No. I will refuse."

William looked at her. "That's a pity."

Gail ignored the obvious compliment.

Helen asked him directly. "Will you do it?"

"Perhaps I'm being thick here, but what's all this about? I've customers I need to serve."

Helen apologized. "Sorry. We should have explained. Gail isn't sure if Adam is serious about her so we thought if he saw someone else invite her out, he might react. You know, show some emotion."

"I see. So I'm supposed to be some kind of stooge. Is that it?"

Helen looked excited. "So you're willing to do this?"

"I'm still trying to understand what you want."

Gail voiced her feelings. "See. I told you he wouldn't want to do it."

"Wrong! I am willing. It could be interesting. But let me get it straight."

William pointed to Helen and asked. "Let me be sure – you're Gail, right?"

"No I'm Helen. She's Gail."

"I was only teasing – of course I know you're Helen." Then turning to Gail he affirmed his understanding, "And you're Gail."

"Yes. And my boyfriend's Adam."

"And you want me to pretend to invite you out at a time when Adam would see us?"

"Yeh. And I'll refuse your invitation." Turning to Helen, Gail again expressed her feelings. "Helen, this sounds really stupid."

William found a slight flaw with the plan. "No, I think it could work, except for one small aspect."

Helen asked. "What's wrong with it?"

William voiced the obvious. "The boys aren't here."

"They should be – they're late."

William raised his eyebrows. "Oh, you mean today?"

Gail agreed. "Yes."

"Ok, then there is an even bigger problem."

Helen's voice displayed her anxiety. "What now?"

"If I were to ask Gail out, I would do it right now. I wouldn't wait 'til the boys were here, would I?"

Gail showed her disbelief in the plan. "No – he's right. This is stupid – let's can this whole idea."

Helen smiled at both of them. "Simple solution. Gail and I will go out quickly right now and hide 'til Adam and Bert come in. Bert's my boyfriend and I know he's totally committed to me so we don't need to involve him. But when we come back in, you can ask Gail."

Gail pointed out. "But we can't come back immediately – it'll look contrived."

William raised his eyebrows. "And this whole charade doesn't look contrived? Hey, if you're going to do this, get out now before they get here. When you come back you can say you were held up in class."

As the two got up and started leaving, Gail agreed. "Good idea. We don't have any classes with them, so they'll not know if it's true."

"Stop chatting, Gail – let's move quickly and get out of here before they arrive."

William spoke quietly. "Don't forget your books."

It was good that William said that because Helen had left her books on the table. She came back and picked them up. "Oops. Thanks – that would have been awkward."

"See you later. I hope I get it right. It's Gail I'm inviting and Adam is the one you're concerned about. And Helen, you and Bert are perfectly matched, right?"

Helen agreed. "That's right – bye for now."

Gail and Helen went quickly out of the cafe and William went back to clearing away dishes and serving other customers.

Part 2

After a few minutes, Adam and Bert entered the cafe and looked around.

Bert spoke loudly. "D'you see the girls anywhere?"

"No."

"Typical. They're late. … Why are women always late?"

Adam looked at his watch and commented. "Actually, Bert, we're late. For all we know they may have come and gone."

"Late? We are men and men don't do late. Time starts when we arrive."

"Look at your watch. Admit it – we're late."

With a customary smirk, Bert replied. "Well, if we're late, then they are even later. So there. Anyway I'm thirsty. Our usual table?"

As they walked over to the table where Gail and Helen had been sitting, they continued their discussion.

Adam made a suggestion. "We could ask if they were here and left."

"Ask who?"

"The waiter, idiot."

"Ah yes." Bert then yelled out. "Garçon!"

Adam looked at Bert with displeasure. "What did you just say?"

"I called the waiter over. It's Italian for waiter and he should know that working here."

"Actually it's French and means 'boy' not waiter."

"Same thing. It's foreign and if you say it loud enough they all understand."

Adam commented on the obvious. "Really? I don't see the waiter coming over."

"I guess he's just an ignorant git. When we call he should come running over if he knows what side of his plate the jam is on."

"Don't you mean which side of his bread the butter's on?"

"Yeh. Yeh, whatever. You call him then – if you're so smart."

Adam raised his hand to attract William's attention. "Excuse me. Have you seen the girls here?"

William replied. "There are lots of girls here. Are you just looking for girls or some specific girls?"

Bert interjected. "Two girls, Helen and Gail. Probably giggling about some stupid TV show they've seen. You know us – we've all been here frequently and you've served us before. So – have they been here today?"

"Oh – now you mention it, you do look familiar. Alan and Bobbie isn't it?"

Bert blistered. "No. Adam and Bert. Bobbie's a girl's name – can't you tell the difference?"

"Sometimes it's difficult the way people dress these days. So again, what was it you wanted to know?"

"Bert, here, was wondering if the two girls we normally come in with have been here today?"

"I've been really busy this shift so I'm not sure."

"Oh well thanks." Turning to his companion he asked. "Bert, why don't we wait and see if they turn up."

"Yeh. Sure. So let's have a drink while we wait – waiter – sir. Can we have some drinks now?"

"I need to know what you want, Tea? Cappuccino? Latte? Espresso?"

Before William could continue, Bert butted in. "What's the difference between Cappuccino and Latte?"

With a serious expression William replied. "Not much really. The machine makes more noise when doing a Latte or perhaps it's the other way round."

Bert did not like the answer. "Smart ass are we? Well I'll have a Canadiano."

"We do an Americano but I don't think we do, what did you say, a Canadiano."

Pleased that William had fallen into his trap, Bert responded. "Oh but you do! Let me explain. Canada is further north than America. Right? And it's colder in Canada than America. Right? When I've ordered an Americano, you're so slow delivering it, it's cold. So by then it's a Canadiano. Right?"

And Bert burst out laughing at his own joke to Adam's embarrassment.

"Funny. Funny, Bert. But I don't think our waiter quite sees it the same way." Turning to William he continued. "Sorry about that. Anyway. I'll have a latte and Bert here will have a hot Americano."

With a slight smile, William accepted their order. "I'll see what I can do for you."

Bert sneered at William. "Yeh. Remember I want it hot. Really hot."

William walked off to get the drinks but he was still within earshot of the boys.

Adam expressed his displeasure. "That was just rude."

Bert huffed back. "Hey lighten up. He's just a dumb waiter. Yeh – a dumb waiter except he goes back and forth instead of up and down like a real dumb waiter?" And he laughed again at his own joke. "D'you get it? Dumb waiter, eh?"

"If he's a dumb waiter, how come he was able to talk to us? Not that dumb eh?"

Bert snarled at Adam. "What's with you? Here we are – the first time we've hung out together without the girls and you're sniping at me as if you're one of them. If it wasn't that we're waiting for them I wouldn't be spending time with you. You're just a bloody bore you are."

"Gail doesn't seem to think so."

"You and Gail? You're a real loser there, Adam."

"I don't think so. Nor does she. And what d'you mean I'm a loser?"

"She's just a blooming swat – that's all. Study – study – study."

"Of course Gail's got a lot of work. She's studying engineering."

"Studying the engineers more likely. Women shouldn't be doing engineering. That's a man's job. Women don't really understand numbers."

"Do you live in this century, Bert?"

"Sure do. It's you who's not. I mean, how many girls you going out with right now?"

"One – Gail! She's the only girl in my life. Why would I go out with others when I've got Gail?"

"And you're sure Gail's not going out with someone else?"

"Absolutely. We agreed on that at the beginning of the year."

Bert laughed. "Yeh. Yeh. Like I agreed the same with Helen. But I'm not sticking to it."

"Well I am. And so is Gail."

Bert smirked at his companion. "And if some girl made a pass at you, you'd turn her down? Really? You'd turn down some sexy wench making eyes at you?"

Adam was becoming annoyed. "Of course I would. I said I'm going out with Gail. No one else."

"And what if someone asked Gail out? What d'you think she'd do?"

"She'd turn them down. This is stupid. Why all the questions?"

"You're sure of that?"

"Sure of what?"

"Sure she'd turn them down."

Adam was becoming even more annoyed. "Yes – I said – that's what we agreed. Only seeing each other – no others."

"So what if dumbo waiter here asked her out?"

"What? Apart from the fact that's highly unlikely to happen, she'd say no."

"Yeh? And what would you feel if someone else invited out your girl, as you put it?"

"I wouldn't be surprised. She's a great girl. But anyway, what did you mean – not sticking to it?"

"Not sticking to what?"

"Only going out with Helen."

"Oh that. Stupid girl actually believes me. That suits me fine as it leaves me free to – well – you know – play the field behind her back."

"Are you saying you're cheating on Helen?"

Bert smiled as he explained. "Of course I am. Let's see. On Tuesdays Helen sits in to watch some stupid TV show so I go out with Clarissa and we have some fun, if you know what I mean. Then sometimes on Thursdays or even Saturdays I make some excuse to Helen and go out with Carol or Dahlia or Trudy."

Adam looked aghast. "Is that it or are there more?"

"Depends who's around."

"And Helen doesn't know anything about this?"

"Of course not. What d'you think I am? Dumb or something like this stupid waiter? Talking of that where is he?" Bert then shouted in a loud voice, "Hey. Garçon! Where's our coffee?"

William replied. "Just coming over Mr Philanderer."

"What did he just call me? I didn't catch it."

Adam attempted not to laugh as he explained. "I think he said Mr Philand. uh. Mr Phil. Mr Philosopher. Yes Mr Philosopher. That's what it must have been."

Bert smiled. "Mr Philosopher. Eh. That's good – describes me perfectly."

William came over with the coffees and emphasizing the word hot, laid their drinks on the table. "Ok guys. Here you are. One latte and one hot Americano."

Bert took a swig of his and yelped out loud. "Wow, that's hot. How'd you get it so hot this time?"

"Oh well that's more of a Mexicano."

"What the hell's that? I asked for a hot Americano!"

William smiled. "That's what you got. Let me explain. Mexico's hotter than America, Right? And you wanted your Americano extra hot. Right? So it's got Mexican hot pepper sauce in it. We call the extra hot Americano a Mexicano. Enjoy your drink."

Bert sneered back. "Ho. Ho. Joke eh? Well the joke's on you dumb ass cause it's actually not that bad."

William walked away smiling smugly.

Adam inquired. "Really – pepper sauce and coffee? And you like it?"

"Absolutely not. It's disgusting but I wasn't going to let him get the better of me, no way. That guy's a real twit – bet he didn't even finish high school."

"Well you better finish it."

"Finish what? High school?"

"Your Mexicano, idiot. You said it was great."

"Hell no. It's awful and burns my mouth."

Adam smiled. "Yeh, but if you don't finish it, he'll have won, won't he?"

"Didn't think of that."

"No, you don't do much thinking."

Bert took another swig and shuddered. "Cheez, this is awful. It's burning my mouth. D'you want to try it?"

"Even though you make it sound so inviting, I don't think so."

"Go on. Have a sip."

"Not after you've been drinking it, thanks."

Bert bridled. "What d'you mean by that?"

"With all the girls you've been going out with? I'm not taking that kind of a risk – no way."

"Girls? Risk? D'you think I'd go out with a girl who had some, uh some STD problem? Is that what you're saying?"

Adam replied calmly. "No. What I said was you don't think. Maybe they do, maybe they don't. How would you know? They're unlikely to tell you are they?"

"Yeh – you got a point there."

Part 3

Bert noticed Gail and Helen come into the cafe and spoke quickly to Adam. "Change the topic. Quickly. The girls are here."

The girls saw the boys, walked over and sat down beside them.

Bert looked at them and snarled. "You're late – as always."

Gail apologized. "Sorry we're a bit late. Class went on a bit long."

Bert sneered. "See what I told you, Adam. Study, study, study! No real social life."

Gail responded angrily. "What d'you mean? We're here aren't we?"

Helen decided to defuse the rising tension. "Hey. I could do with a drink. I see you guys didn't wait for us."

Adam answered. "The drinks have only just arrived. Latte and cappuccino as usual for you two?"

They both nodded in agreement.

Adam called William over. "Waiter! Can we order for the girls now please?"

William walked over, looked at Helen and began speaking. "Helen?"

Gail looked surprised, "Don't you mean Gail. I'm Gail."

William shook his head. "No, I know you're Gail. It's Helen I'm surprised to see."

Helen's face showed concern that William was getting the plan entirely wrong. "I'm sure you mean Gail."

"No. No. Come on Helen. You can't have forgotten Tuesday already."

Helen was stunned by this comment. "Tuesday? I. I don't know what you mean."

William continued. "When we were … well you know."

At this point Bert interjected. "What the hell's going on here? Tuesday? What's with Tuesday? Helen! You said you watch TV on Tuesdays."

"Yeh I do and I don't know what William is meaning."

Bert was beginning to show annoyance. "Oh *'William'* is it? I come here nearly every day but don't know his name but you do? First name basis, eh?"

Gail tried to correct the obvious misunderstanding. "Yes of course, we all do. We all know his name. – at least all of us who listen and care."

Then turning to William she tried to get his attention. "But William, I'm sure you've got this wrong. Why are you talking about Helen? Are you sure you mean Helen?"

William smiled again. "Hey. There are some things one can forget and other things one remembers. Helen and Tuesdays? I'm unlikely to forget."

Bert bristled. "Just what are you insinuating?"

Looking straight at Bert, William pulled the pin out of a verbal grenade. "Well on Tuesdays do you think Helen spends all her time watching TV? On the evenings when you're out with, what's her name – Clarie?"

Without thinking, Bert immediately corrected William. "Her name's Clarissa. She hates being called Clarie."

Gail and Helen turned and stared at Bert. There was silence until Helen spoke out. "How d'you know what name she hates?"

Slightly flustered Bert blurted out. "Adam must have told me."

Adam objected. "Don't pin that on me. Before today I'd never even heard of this Clarissa you're seeing on Tuesdays."

Bert pleaded. "Come on Adam. You're supposed to be a friend."

Helen jumped in. "Clarissa? On Tuesdays? But we agreed. You said you're only seeing me. Just me. You said you go out with the boys on Tuesdays."

"Yeh. Yeh. I do."

Bert pointed to William and continued. "What this guy's saying is pure lies."

William was enjoying this discussion. "Does that mean Trudy and Carol don't exist? I thought you said they were for Thursdays and Saturdays?"

Bert snarled at William. "Stay out of this dumbo, if you know what's good for you. Get back to your coffee grinder before I put you through it."

In a cold voice Helen asked. "Who are Trudy and Carol?"

William risked another word. "You asking me or Bert?"

In an increasingly cold voice Helen asked again. "I'm asking Bert. Who are Trudy and Carol?"

William decided to retreat and go back to serving customers as Bert began scrambling for help. "Listen Helen. Walter, William, or whatever his name is – he's just making up lies. All lies. There is no Trudy or Carol. Come on Adam. Help me out here – tell Helen the truth."

Adam declined with growing disgust. "From what I understand, William did quite a good job with telling the truth."

Helen asked again. "Truth? Bert I want the truth from you. Why has William mentioned a Clarissa and a Trudy and a Carol?"

Bert tried to back track. "Come on babe. We can work this out."

"Don't *'babe'* me. Work what out? You just said it was all lies."

Bert changed his tone. "Be realistic Helen. You think you're the only girl I'm going out with?"

"That's what you told me. That's what we agreed. What the hell have you been playing at?"

"Well I'm not saintly like Adam here."

Adam did not appreciate this comment. "What d'you mean by that?"

Bert turned to Adam and sneered. "You and Gail. What did you say? *'Only girl in my life.'* You're a loser Adam. You're missing out. Personally, I wouldn't go out with Gail, even if you paid me."

Gail spoke with repulsion. "Don't worry. I wouldn't go out with you. In fact I'd stay far away from you. I've heard about Carol and it's now probably not just your mind that's diseased."

That comment had Bert's attention. "What d'you mean you've heard about Carol? What have you heard? What's this about disease?"

Gail smirked. "You'll find out soon enough."

Helen was beginning to understand the situation. "And might I ask, why you are concerned about Carol's health? Especially if all this is just lies?"

There was a long silence and she continued. "Lies? No. I can see now the lies have been those you've been telling me."

Bert tried a different approach. "Come on Helen. Let's go somewhere else and work this out. Let's not lose what we have."

Helen's eyes grew smaller and with a sharp tone she told him exactly what she thought. "What we have? Let me tell you – WE have nothing. As of now there is no WE and you're right – it's about time you left but I'm not going with you. Not now. Not ever again. The only working out to be done is me trying to work out why I ever trusted you."

Bert rose to leave. "Ok have it your way but you'll regret it. You'll be back. You'll come crawling back to me on your hands and knees. You'll see. Ok. Let's go Adam. We need to leave these —"

Before Bert could finish his sentence, Adam interrupted him. "No Bert. You're on your own. I don't associate with pillocks like you."

"What? What are you saying? You're not siding with these stupid girls are you? We go back a long way, Adam. Come on, we're leaving now, you and I."

Adam shook his head. "No. We don't go back a long way. Today was the first time we hung out together without the girls and from what I've heard from you today, I'm not doing that again, Bert. In words you can understand – get lost and don't look upon me as a friend."

Helen chimed in. "Or me. I don't want to see you ever again."

Bert leaned over to her. "Don't say something you'll regret, Helen. I'll call you later when you've calmed down."

Helen looked sternly back at him. "Listen carefully, Bert. If you call me or text me, I'll bring a charge against you for harassment and stalking. Get out of here. It's not even goodbye. It's just good riddance."

Bert kicked his chair and left mumbling under his breath. "See if I care. There're many fish in the sea."

After a moment of silence, Gail turned to Helen. "Well that didn't quite go to plan did it?"

"No. Not according to plan but perhaps for the better."

Adam looked from one to the other. "What plan? What are you talking about?"

Helen was about to speak when Gail glanced at her with a stern look and then smiled at Adam. "Oh just girl talk, dear. Nothing to worry about."

She then turned to her friend. "What were we saying earlier about Tom?"

Before Helen could respond Adam asked with a worried look on his face. "Who's Tom? What's going on here today?"

Both girls laughed as Helen explained. "Tom is a nasty character in the soap I've been watching. He's been two timing his supposed girlfriend. Sound familiar?"

Adam thought it best to agree. "Oh. I see. Truth weirder than fiction – is that it?"

"That kind of thing." She then turned to Gail and asked. "You said you'd heard about Carol? Who is she? What have you heard?"

Gail smiled. "I don't know any Carol and haven't heard anything about a Carol. I just said it to see Bert's reaction."

"Well you sure got one. If he's worried about her then I'm well rid of him. Thanks Gail. His reaction helped me decide to dump him."

"Yeh. I thought it might. Well, I've probably had enough for today. I don't really feel like a coffee now. Shall we go?"

Helen declined. "No not me. You two go off. I just want to sit here on my own for a while. … No really. … On you go. And thanks Adam – for being a true friend to Gail and me."

As Adam and Gail got up to leave he replied. "I didn't know any of that about Bert 'til today. I can assure you – he's not someone I'll be spending time with again. You ready Gail?"

Adam picked up Gail's books to her surprise. "You carrying my books?"

"Yeh. It's the least I can do."

She was appreciative. "Thanks. Reminds me of high school." She then turned to Helen. "You sure you're ok on your own?"

"I just need some time to think. But thanks."

"See you later then. Bye."

Part 4

After Gail and Adam left, Helen sat staring at nothing for a long time. William was near the exit preparing something as she called out. "William?"

He came over looking slightly apprehensive and as he began clearing up the dirty cups, he started to speak. "I'm —"

But Helen interrupted him. "What happened? You were supposed to come over and invite Gail out? Where did all that stuff about going out with me and seeing me come from? As far as I know we've never been out together? So please explain."

133

"I never actually said we went out. I was very careful in my words just to plant questions in Bert's mind."

"But why? And where did Clarissa and the others come from? Given his reaction, what you said obviously hit a nerve and must've had some truth to it. But how did you know any of it? You never said anything about that when we talked earlier."

"People often think of waiters as robots bringing drinks and taking away dirty dishes. But we have ears. We hear much more than people realize."

"Were you eavesdropping on them?"

"Well not actually eavesdropping. You and Gail asked me to do something weird and I was just gathering background information."

"Are you saying Bert spoke about Clarissa, Carol and whatever her name is just before we came in?"

"Spoke? No. Boasted would be a better word. Berating Adam for being faithful and attached to Gail. I could see there was no need to follow the plan and pretend to ask Gail out. Adam was becoming quite upset with Bert's casual attitude towards his relationship with you."

"So you decided to intervene? Break up me and Bert? Is that it?"

"Um. I suppose you could look at it that way. But in my defence, I knew what you and Gail had been saying about you and Bert and it was obvious you didn't realize what Bert was doing. I'm sorry. I did it to save you from Bert. ... Perhaps I shouldn't have said anything."

"Hey. Don't be sorry, I'm not mad at you. In fact, the exact opposite. I should be saying thanks – you opened my eyes. From what I've learned today, Bert's dead history now. ... No really – I mean thanks."

"As the saying goes – All's well that end's well?"

"Something like that. Out of interest, do you listen in on everybody's conversations? Do all waiters do that?"

William paused then replied. "Admission time. Being a waiter is a critical aspect of my course work. I'm doing a masters degree in social psychology and working here's part of my research project."

"Psychology? Did you say psychology?"

"Yes. Social psychology."

"What's your last name?"

"Kendle. Why?"

"You're William Kendle?"

"Last time I looked, yes."

"You tutor one of the senior psychology classes don't you?"

"Guilty as charged. Again why?"

"My friend Katherine's in your group and keeps talking about you. I think she's got a crush on you and I can see why. You should ask her out."

And then in a different tone after a slight pause. "Or perhaps you're attached to someone?"

William shook his head. "No. Not attached. No one even on the horizon. I know who you mean but I couldn't ask her out. College rules. We're not allowed to fraternize with our students."

Helen looked at him for a long moment and decided to take the risk. "Not allowed to go out with your students? Eh?" She then looked straight at William's eyes and after another long pause and with a growing smile commented, "Well, I'm not one of your students."

William took another long moment before replying. "I know. Perhaps that's a good thing. Is it?"

She let the silence linger, tipped her head slightly and replied in a soft voice. "Could be —— what d'you think?"

He returned the look. "What do I think? Well, my shift here ends in twenty minutes. D'you want a coffee now. Or – shall we have one together – later – somewhere else?"

With a cheeky grin she enquired, "Can I have both?"

"You sure can. Your normal Cappuccino? Right?"

Helen paused. "No. This time I'll have an Americano please."

"Ok. One normal Americano coming up."

"Normal? Are there different kinds of Americano?"

William looked at her. "I'll tell you later and you know what? — it might even make you smile."

Author's Note

This story was originally conceived as a one act short play. As such it is included in the collection of short plays *'Story & Script Vol 1'*.

A HORTICULTURAL CONUNDRUM

Rabbit sat back in his chair and took a puff at his pipe.

"You say you're growing weeds?"

"Yes," chirped back Mouse. "I was growing flowers but the weeds were doing better and had some lovely blooms so I decided to take out all the flowers and now I'm making a great garden just of weeds."

"Mmmm." Rabbit took another puff at his pipe.

"You know you can't do that," he said.

Mouse responded indignantly. "Why not? I am and it looks beautiful."

"You may think you are, but since a weed by definition is an unwanted plant it is logically impossible to cultivate weeds. Your weeds are now flowers and your flowers have become weeds."

Mouse furrowed his eyebrows, crinkled his whiskers and tried hard to think, but summer was not a good time for logic or thinking. So with barely a goodbye, he scurried off back to his garden to water his weeds – or as Rabbit had put it – his flowers – which had been weeds until he liked them.

And then he looked at the lovely white blossom on the bindwee … bind … bind … bindflower?

It was all far too confusing for a little mouse.

DOWN BUT NOT GONE

In June each year we make sure we are there – on Gold Beach – that stretch of the Normandy coast used by the British forces during the D-Day invasion of Europe. When I say I am there, you will not be able to see me as Gold Beach is where I ceased to exist as a physical person. But I can assure you, I am there.

On the morning of 6 June 1944, I landed along with others and we took up positions on the beach. We fired shots and were fired upon. Suddenly a shell landed almost on top of me obliterating all evidence of my existence except for my dog tags. When the body boys came by the following day all they could find were the two identification discs which showed my name, service number and blood type – not that the latter was now of any value. They recorded the details so those back in England could be informed. I had listed Florence, my fiancée, as my next of kin.

Being no longer constrained by the limitations of physical existence, I made sure I was present when the telegram boy rang the door bell of our little thatched cottage outside Dorchester. Before even opening the dreaded telegram, Florence began trembling and crying as she knew what it would say. I watched and if I had real eyes, they would have been overflowing with tears for her grief.

As spirits, we, the departed, are basically just wisps of energy. Sometimes we can change our energy so that light passing through us is dispersed like mist. Some people refer to this effect as 'seeing a ghost'.

Much though I loved Florence, I made the decision not to reveal my presence. To have done so could have affected her life forever afterwards. She would always have wondered if I was there and perhaps have felt guilty about forming another loving relationship. My love for Florence was too strong to let me impose such a burden on her. So I left and have never gone back lest by accident I might reveal my presence.

In June we do not reveal ourselves but our energy is felt. Oft we hear people on the beach whispering a hushed acknowledgement, "This place is special – you can almost feel the presence of those who gave their lives for the sake of others."

With due respect, I wish I could point out to these people that we did not *'give our lives'* – they were brutally taken from us. But that is the nature of war — take or be taken – and my life was taken. I hold no grudge against the Germans who loaded and fired the gun – had I been them I would have done the same for my own self preservation.

So now, every June, I and my fellow spirits patrol the beaches trying to impress upon visitors the carnage of war and the importance of peace. You may not see us —— but we are there. *Down but not gone.*

THAT GUY

As they sat down with their cappuccinos, Sandra leant over to Aileen and started a conversation. "You know that guy I mentioned."

"D'you mean your new neighbour? The dream man in the 'no-go zone'?"

"Yeh. Well. We went out for dinner yesterday and he's a really nice guy."

"Oh Sandra – what are you doing? After your last relationship crisis, I thought you swore to stick to single guys and never dip into the 'no-go zone' of attached men again. But here you go, charging into that zone. So what happened to his lady friend? — Did she go out with you as well? — A happy threesome?"

It had only been a few weeks since the new neighbour moved into the empty apartment on Sandra's floor. Even if Sandra had not been single, she would still have noticed him. He was hard to ignore. Tall, blonde haired, well tanned and with a smile to dream about. And she did.

There was, though, just one small problem. Actually, not that small – the woman who was living with him. When Sandra came home from work, she often saw the lady leaving his apartment, dressed to kill. Hair done to perfection, makeup applied without overstatement, a figure hugging evening dress and sparkling Jimmy Choo type shoes.

Late at night, Sandra often heard the high heel stutter going back into his apartment. With a touch of envy she felt some girls have it all and to top it off, this annoying lady had her neighbour.

Sandra replied, "No. It was just the two of us for dinner."

"Go on. He said she was his sister or cousin or some other slippery line. — And you fell for it? Sandra you're hopeless."

Sandra was enjoying this. "No nothing like that. It was all perfectly above board and respectable. When he asked me out I mentioned the lady living in his apartment and he just laughed."

"Laughed? … And you still went out with him?"

"Yes. There is no lady – he's an out of work actor and for work right now, he dresses like a lady and works in a local bar. But I can assure you – that's not him. Let me tell you – he can move in with me any time."

CONTACT BX5

Amelia thumbed through the local newspaper looking for inspiration. The tutor of her class on creative writing had set a specific task – write an opening paragraph for a short story based on something you read in the newspaper. What could be simpler? But by page 27, Amelia had found nothing to spark her imagination. Then came page 28 – the 'Lonely Hearts' section. She had recently taken to reading the entries.

Her two year engagement to Stanley had been doomed from the start and Amelia was glad to be free. His interests were centred on strenuous outdoor activities – rugby, mountaineering, cross country running. She preferred a quieter life – coffee shops, reading and writing. She knew the relationship had no future when he disparagingly scorned her interests claiming that *'story writers are just people afraid of reality'*. She then showed him reality – she kicked him out and enrolled in a creative writing class.

It was a small group – two men, three women and a tutor of indeterminate gender. The discussion sessions were both challenging and entertaining but revealed little about their personal lives. After all it was supposed to be about creative writing not memoir revelations.

Her scanning of page 28 stopped abruptly. Her eyes opened wide and she re-read the entry. *'Engagement ring – recently polished – ready for use'*.

Forgetting why she was reading the paper, Amelia's devilish streak came to the fore. The paper ran a completely confidential process – the replies and correspondence were always double blind using only a registration number. She had registered shortly after Stanley's departure but had never replied to anything. She smiled and thought – *why not have some fun?*

In an outer envelope addressed to the newspaper Amelia put another envelope showing the details of the person she was replying to – Contact BX5. On plain paper she had written just one line — '*Ring finger – recently emptied*'.

Getting back to the task in hand, on a later page Amelia found a news item with potential – '*Sailing yacht somersaults after hitting submerged rock*'. After many attempts to construct a suitable paragraph, Amelia admitted defeat.

Anyway what did she know about sailing? Near the end of their relationship, Stanley had persuaded her to go on a sailing trip with those reassuring words, "You will enjoy it." But her concept of enjoyment did not include being sick in the boat, sick on the shore and increasingly sick of him. The memory was so unpleasant she put down her pencil, closed the newspaper and postponed the writing to another day.

Coming home from work later that week she found a letter on the doormat marked '*From BX5*'. She had not expected a reply but perhaps this was an invite – a suggestion of where they could meet. Ripping it open her initial reaction was one of disappointment and then bewilderment. A simple slip of paper with two words – *What size*?

What size? What size of what? Ah yes – her finger. Her previous message had referred to her ring finger. Two can play this came. Inner envelope, outer envelope stamped ready to be posted and deep inside she had written her two word response — *What colour?*

A few days later another envelope from BX5. Surely a sensible answer this time – but no. '*Daffodil Blue*' was what she read. No other words – just '*Daffodil Blue*'. But daffodils are never blue – they can be yellow – they can even be white but never blue. Perhaps it was time to shut down this exchange. What sort of nut dreams up such a stupid colour?

She then realized that perhaps she had enough for her writing exercise. Yes – this had all the hallmarks of a love story. If she could not live it in reality, she could at least live it in her imagination. Draft after draft ensued. But Amelia's romantic streak kept taking her past the opening paragraph with flights of fancy about them meeting and falling in love.

What had Lee, the tutor, said? "One opening paragraph."

One paragraph – that's all. No one needs to know what a fool I have been. So Amelia penned a simple opening, stopping before it became unbelievable.

At these writing classes someone was chosen to read out their work and the others commented, with guidance from Lee. By a throw of dice, tonight was Amelia's turn. With half suppressed amusement she read her work out loud.

> *Nancy always read the 'Personal' column partially out of enjoyment and partially out of searching and hoping. This week she felt she had to laugh at the entry* 'Engagement ring – recently polished – ready for use'. *Still laughing she penned a reply in the same style and marked it – 'Confidential – not for publication'. She had written* 'Ring finger – recently emptied'.

When she finished reading to the group, there were controlled giggles from the girls, a distinct 'oooh' from Lee and the men wore bland expressions which could be interpreted as 'not another silly love story'.

Lee looked around. "Gerald, let's start with you tonight. What do you think?"

"What do I think? Not much really. The sentence structure's ok but the story's not going anywhere. I know this is a creative writing class but this is too far – no one would act that way. No; it's just not believable."

Amelia held her tongue (*You ain't seeing half of it!*)

Sheila could not contain herself, "No – no, Gerald. This opening has all sorts of possibilities. Where do they meet? Are they compatible? Come on, let your mind flow – be human."

Candice chimed in. "I'm with Sheila – what a romantic response *'ring finger recently emptied?'* I wish I had the courage to reply like that. Why did you stop there? What do you think happens next, Amelia?"

Amelia muttered to herself – *If you knew you wouldn't believe it.*

She was saved from an embarrassing admission by Lee's interjection, "Robert, you are being quiet this evening. What do you feel?"

Robert paused before responding and his words were baffling to all but one. Staring directly at Amelia he uttered just two words. "What size?"

Amelia was not sure if her heart had stopped or exploded. (*Robert? What size? Robert – the person she looked forward to seeing at these classes? Was Robert BX5? This could not be happening. What could she possibly say now?*) But before her mind could calm down she had blurted out, "What colour?"

The others glanced in turn between Robert and Amelia, trying without success to understand the meaning behind these cryptic exchanges. While all the time Robert sat back in his chair, chin supported in his hand, finger on his nose.

Amelia's heart was now in overdrive (*come on, Robert, you know the next line*). But without expression Robert threw a dagger – a sharp, pointed, penetrating dagger, "I could say Sunrise Red."

(*Red? No, not red. Oh why red? You know it was not red.*) This time her heart, her breathing, her excitement – all stopped. Amelia felt her face deflate as she bit her lip to prevent her eyes from watering. Her mind was in turmoil (W*hy did you say red? I was so enjoying these classes and your company – how can I come back here again? Red? Oh how cruel.*) But she said nothing – there was nothing she could say.

Robert had always been attracted to Amelia but had never wanted to upset the dynamics of the group by asking her out. He studied her reaction but not for long. Her obvious disappointment and her down turned eyes told him all he needed to know and with a warm smile, he withdrew the dagger.

"Amelia, if it's what you'd like – I'd be very happy to change that to a colour we both know. What would you say to Daffodil Blue?"

Her face lit up, "I'd like that."

"And if I suggested dinner for two?"

"I'd like that even more."

GIVING IN

The man sitting opposite me at the table looked like a poster for a Frankenstein horror film. His eyes were evil – his face was evil – even his stance oozed evilness. And he was not alone. Standing behind him smirking and glaring alternately was a compact fireball of a lady. A lady? No. Perhaps describing her just as a repulsive person of indeterminate gender would be more appropriate.

The man, referred to only as Kobe the Knife, suddenly stood up with a violent motion which shook the air in the room. As if I was not yet petrified enough, he brought his fist down hard on the table with a resounding thump which caused the table to bounce and tremble. However, the table's trembling was nothing compared to the fear-induced jiggering of my limbs. How could these people think it was acceptable to cause such anxiety?

With his fists clenched and his arms shaking he uttered a guttural groan. "You know it has to be done our way." His words echoed back and forth off the sterile walls of what felt like a torture chamber.

The fireball woman merely grinned and nodded agreement as in a much softer but more sinister tone she gurgled a warning. "If you don't do it our way, you'll regret it and I'll enjoy seeing you squirm." At this point her hands floated over the instruments of torture laid out on the still shaking table.

There was a dull edged knife – the kind you'd find in a dining room cutlery drawer. Apparently it is much more painful to be sliced and slashed with a dull knife. Beside it was a small spoon covered in a sticky looking red gunge. I'd read how gangsters use such an implement to gouge out the eyes of recalcitrant obstinate objectors. They obviously saw me as one and a silly thought scurried across my brain – both eyes or just one.

He saw me eyeing the tools. "I see you've noticed – you won't be the first to attempt to defy us and you won't be the last. Fasasa, this charming lady beside me, is an expert at using these. She learned at a young age from her father exactly how it should be done to create maximum pain. Although I hate watching pain, it won't really affect me — because you're the one who'll *feel* the pain."

Then in a more sinister whisper he added, "You'll understand the true meaning of pain if you don't do it the way we tell you. There are two ways to do it and your way – is wrong."

Fasasa, the compact fireball, spoke again. "You may think you know but as Knife-man Kobe said, you are wrong, wrong, wrong. You must do it the way we dictate or there'll be consequences and consequences means a mess."

She paused. Then with a high pitch banshee scream, she fair flew over to my side of the table and changing her countenance began a mesmerizing chant. "Do it our way. Do it our way. Stop thinking your way is right. Do it our way. Do it our way."

I was almost on the point of giving in and doing it the way they insisted even if only to release me from this torment but NO. I was not going to give in and told them so in as many words.

"I will not do it your way. I'll continue to do it my way so stop trying to change my life. I've said it before and I'll say it again. The jam has always got to go on the scone BEFORE the clotted cream."

Many British restaurant goers (and American tourists) are fond of the afternoon specialty referred to as a Dorset Cream Tea (sometimes referred to as a Devon Cream Tea by residents of that county). Apart from the tea, the delicacy consists of a scone, a container of jam (preferably strawberry) and a container of clotted cream. Although the ingredients are not subject to dispute, there is strong disagreement with respect to the order in which the cream and jam are put on the scone - perhaps, though, not as violently as portrayed in this tale !

MY FIRST JOB

You want to know about my first job? Oooh, that goes back a long way. I think it must have been mid sixties, perhaps '64 or '65 when I was still a young kid in my teens.

I'd been sittin' in the bay window at home wonderin' if I'd ever get a job when Dillon sez to me, "Louie, you gotta break out of your shell and become a real man."

Dillon was my brother, see, and I looked up to him. Well not actually looked up 'cause he was slightly smaller than me, if you knows what I mean, so when I says I looked up to him, I mean I admired him, like. So when he said he needed me, well 'course I rose to the challenge.

He was doin' somethin' with Leroy, his friend, a big guy with arms like tree trunks. I always wished I could look like Leroy. But he spent many hours in the boxin' gym and I weren't allowed there.

Anyways where was I? Oh yeah, Dillon said he and Leroy had some things to iron out first, but I had to be ready Friday evenin' dressed warmly with a dark jacket and thick gloves. He said I had to wear dark even though he knew I only had one warm coat and it were black. Guess he were just bein' cautious.

So on Friday night we all jumps into Leroy's pick-up truck. I think it were a Ford but that don't really matter; it were a pick-up and that's what was important. So off we goes into the countryside, me wonderin' what kind of job this was at night in the country. Then Leroy turns off the highway, goes up a dirt track and stops in the middle of nowhere. I didn't understand but then this was my first job so I just keeps quiet.

I remember Leroy then spoke somethin' like, "The trees are just over the fence. The farmer's already cut 'em and stacked 'em neat, like. Stupid guy. By time he notices, we'll have sold 'em all in the market. Maeve says there's a real shortage of Christmas trees this year in Sherbourne so we should have no trouble gettin' rid of 'em there. But come on. We can't stay here too long, someone may find us."

Bein' the smallest one, they hoists me over the fence and my job was to hand up the trees to Dillon who passed 'em to Leroy who put 'em on the truck. Xmas trees is prickly so I sees why Dillon said to wear thick gloves.

We was doin' fine 'til two police cars came racin' down the road from each direction and blocked us in, like and we was caught. Since it were my first conviction, I gets a suspended sentence – the other two done three months inside. So that was my first job. D'you wanta know about the second one? I got two years for it.

When Jazmin finished typing up her fictional story and handed it to the editor, she was concerned when he called her into his office less than an hour later.

"Jazmin, I liked your piece and I'm pleased to say we'll use it on page five in the *Seasonal Fiction Section*. Keep thinking up stories like that – it's one of the things we hoped you could do when we hired you. And you kept it under 500 words? Well done – for your first job."

A TEMPORAL CONUNDRUM

Crow always enjoyed his discussions with Rabbit who would sit in his reclining deck-chair while Crow fretted around, stomping on the ground to frighten off the smaller birds of which he was afraid.

This time they were exploring *Time and the Meaning of Life* or was it *Life and the Meaning of Time*. It probably did not matter which, as they basically saw little difference between the two thoughts.

It was Crow who had raised the topic with his contentious statement that he was living in the future, not the present. Rabbit had furrowed his nose and refilled his pipe before asking for an explanation.

Crow obliged. "Well, yesterday I said *'I'll talk to Rabbit tomorrow'* and since I am doing that now, this must be tomorrow which is in the future, so I am now living in the future."

Weasel, who had been digging a small hole in the lawn looked up and countered Crow's assertion. "Yes, maybe. But what if you had said *'I'll talk to Rabbit on Friday'* and since today is presently Friday you would be living in today which is the present, not the future. So are you living simultaneously in the future and the present?"

Rabbit lit his pipe from the rays of the sun using a pocket magnifying glass before contributing to this temporal exchange. "Sorry, you two – we always live in the past – not even the present and certainly not the future – always the past."

Weasel, not wanting to appear a total ignoramus, claimed he understood when in fact it was blatantly obvious he didn't. So in an attempt to hide his confusion, Weasel suggested Rabbit explain — "Purely for Crow's benefit."

"Well," said Rabbit, "if you are aware of what you are doing, then you have already done it – even if it is only a micro-second before. Since the brain takes a finite time to process information with respect to what you are doing, you cannot be aware of what you are doing – only what you have done. And when we talk about what we HAVE done that refers to the past — so it follows we only ever *live* in the past."

Before Crow's brain became too muddled, he decided to fly away unsure whether he was doing so in the future, the present or the past.

Weasel nodded sagely as he went back to his digging all the while muttering to himself – *does that mean I should look forward to the past?*

It was not uncommon for discussions with Rabbit to end in such perplexity.

Author's Note

I did not come across the concept underlying this story (that we always *'live'* in the past) by reading tomes on Time Management. No - this was an unprompted philosophical pronouncement made one day by my then ten year old grandson, Calum. With a mind like that, one wonders what he will achieve in the future, which of course, by his determination — will be in the past.

FANTASTIC

It had been many years since Matilda and Sophie had spent time together. At junior high school, even though Matilda had always been a flashy fanciful one, they had been virtually inseparable. However, when Matilda's family moved to a different part of Chicago their friendship waned. For a while they telephoned to keep in contact but soon that stopped as each found new friends.

Sophie pursued her interest in painting and after art college one of the important galleries began exhibiting her work. When her first major one-person show was advertised in the newspaper, she was surprised to receive a message from the gallery saying that a Matilda Frasenheim had called, left her number and could Sophie call her back. Although the surname was different, Sophie felt it must be her old school friend so she called and Matilda answered.

"Oh Sophie, thanks for calling back. It's so nice to hear from you. It's been so long. And I've really missed you, dear."

"Yeah, it's been a long time."

"I so much want to catch up with you. I've got so much to tell you, dear. Shall we meet for coffee? How about Forty Carrots at Bloomingdales?"

Sophie knew this was not the cheapest place to have coffee but if that was where Matilda wanted to go, then so be it.

"Fine – sounds good. Tomorrow? 10 o'clock?"

"Oh sorry, dear, can't do then, I've my yoga meditation class at that time."

"You're doing yoga? Hey, that's fantastic."

Sophie remembered Matilda's distaste for anything requiring effort – she must have really changed and this was worth seeing.

"Oh yes. It's so refreshing and helps calm my inner persona. Thursday would be fine. I won't be chairing the meeting of the Help for Homeless till the afternoon so 10 would be perfect. I'm so tied up with committees today can I leave you to reserve a table, dear? See you then. Bye, darling."

Before Sophie could reply, Matilda had hung up.

Reserve a table? Sophie knew that probably meant she would be expected to pick up the bill but she could not back out now.

On Thursday, it was almost a quarter past ten before Matilda swept into the restaurant all smiles and glitter.

"Oh so good to see you again Sophie, dear. You're looking so well. How do you do it? No don't tell me – it would make me jealous. But then I don't really need to be jealous do I? Not with the way life's been treating me, dear."

Sophie leant back in her chair to reduce the chance of asphyxiation from Matilda's overpowering cheap perfume – it certainly was not one Sophie would buy.

With hardly a pause for breath, Matilda took command of the conversation. "I see you've got an art show coming up. That's so clever of you, dear. I'm so looking forward to seeing it. As you know, I love art."

Based on her memory of Matilda, Sophie was slightly lost for words at this unexpected revelation about art and so just replied with a single word. "Fantastic."

"Herbert taught me all about art."

"Herbert? Is he your husband?"

"Oh yes, dear. Herbert's my darling husband. He's a doctor, you know."

Matilda's words came out so fast, Sophie had little time to respond. She remembered it was best not to interrupt Matilda so Sophie spoke the first word that came into her mind and uttered another quick 'Fantastic'.

"He's a heart specialist. Much in demand."

Sophie was able to slip in another 'Fantastic' before Matilda continued her on-going gurgle of words.

"It meant we had to move out to Magnificent Mile."

"Really? The expensive suburb? Fantastic."

"Oh yes. We needed more space for the cars and for Carson and Penelope."

"Carson and Penelope? Are they your kids?"

"Oh no dear, we haven't time for kids. No – Carson is our butler and Penelope looks after the housekeeping staff."

"What can I say but how great for you. I knew this would happen to you one day – it's just fantastic."

"I know. Carson would have driven me here today in the Bentley but it's in for service so we had to use the Lincoln."

"It must be great to have such helpful people around you."

"Oh yes – you can't imagine how much I rely on them, especially on golf days."

"You play golf as well? That's fantastic."

"Oh I don't just play – I'm also vice-chair of the social committee. You know what it's like."

"I don't, actually, but in your case I can imagine. Vice-chair? Fantastic. I can see you being chair one day."

"Oh thanks, dear – I will make a great chairperson, won't I? But oh Sophie, dear. I've been spending all our time here talking about my little hum-drum life and there you are doing such great things with, er … art. Tell me how did it all begin? Tell me everything. Make me jealous."

"Well – after high school my parents sent me to a finishing school in Switzerland."

"A finishing school? In Switzerland? Did they speak English? What kind of things do they teach at a finishing school? Did you learn anything there?"

"They taught us how to be polite in company."

"Oh tell me more dear. What was the most important thing you learned?"

"Well ... one of the things they taught us was – in polite company, don't use the word bullshit – instead, just say – fantastic."

For some reason, at that point Matilda stood up and walked out.

THE BOX

"Mr Kirkwood. If you'd like to come this way, Ken Parson is waiting for you at Table 20."

Geoff picked up the old writing box and cradling it in his arms he followed the lady to Table 20.

Just before his mother passed away, she'd asked Geoff to do two things for her – just two. Firstly, look after her young dog and secondly, take care of the old French writing box. She claimed they could both change his life and without explanation she made him promise to carry out her wishes. He told her to rest assured that he would do as she requested. He could hardly do otherwise during her final days.

Fortunately he liked dogs. He just didn't like the name his mother had given to this dog – *Marie*. Nobody calls their dog Marie, even if it's female. Whenever he had asked her why, she claimed the dog was named after the *Marie Celeste* because when very young, Marie kept disappearing. Geoff knew this could not be the real reason but Mum had insisted so the story stuck and so did the name.

His mother had said Marie would change his life and in that she was correct. Just a few days after Marie came to live in Geoff's house, his partner, Henrietta, screamed at him, "You love that damned dog more than you love me."

Geoff chose not to comment whereupon Henrietta charged upstairs, packed her bags and flew out of the house to find another man to annoy. That evening Marie earned an extra helping of her favourite dog biscuits.

Marie was a lovely fluffy little Havanese and didn't seem perturbed or embarrassed by her name, unlike Geoff who had found the name acutely embarrassing. One day he had been walking Marie in the special dog zone on the beach when she had run off. So in a loud voice, the kind you need to use when calling a dog, he'd yelled. "Marie! Marie! Come here this minute. If you don't come right now you won't get any biscuits." As dogs do, she ignored his command.

However a lady standing nearby looked directly at Geoff and started laughing. "I assume you have a dog called Marie? The reason I'm laughing is my name is Marie but I don't normally respond to the promise of biscuits."

Geoff felt so embarrassed. "Yes, it's my dog, well actually it was my mother's dog. I didn't give her that name and oh I'm sorry, I dreaded this would happen sometime. Please – accept my apologies."

"No apology needed. I rather enjoyed it – no man has yelled at me that way for many years. Think nothing of it."

It would have been easier for Geoff to think nothing of it if he didn't keep seeing this lady walking her dog on the beach. They often passed each other and exchanged a quick smile and chuckle. She had even taking to stopping some times and asking if Marie had become any more obedient. Her dog was an American Water Spaniel with the much more respectable name of Angus. Not usual but at least a more suitable name for a dog.

When Geoff bought one of those excellent ball throwing things – the ones that mean you don't need to pick up the slithery saliva coated ball with your hands – Marie had enquired where he'd got it and was it worthwhile. Soon she had one as well and they frequently met and together they would throw balls for the dogs. Geoff began realizing he looked forward to these meetings and that he would like to spend more time with Marie, the person, and perhaps less with Marie, the dog.

But did this gorgeous lady with the wind blown blonde hair have a partner or perhaps even a husband? He did not want to destroy these beach side encounters with such a pointed enquiry. Anyway you can hardly say to an attractive woman, "Hey, you've the same name as my bitch here – would you like to go for dinner?" As a chat-up line, he thought it might not be successful.

So instead, he just made sure every day he took Marie for very long walks on the beach. And he kept telling himself it was purely, of course, for Marie's well being – she needed the exercise.

But not today. Today he was at the Antiques Fair and all because of Sarah, his assistant at work. In normal office chit-chat he had asked her if she was doing anything exciting at the weekend.

"Yeh – I'm going to the Antiques Fair in Croman Hall on Sunday."

"Antiques Fair? I didn't know you collected antiques. Will there be many stalls?"

"No – it's not a sale. It's kind of like those antique shows you see on TV where someone brings along something that looks worthless only to find it's worth thousands. You know the kind."

"This Sunday, you say. Do you have to book ahead?"

"No – don't think so. The poster just said turn-up with something interesting and we'll look at it. Why – do you have something?"

"Could be – my mother left me an old writing box – French I think. But it's probably not worth anything."

"Hey – it's free. You might as well try. Perhaps I'll see you there?"

"Yeh, maybe – I'll think about it."

That evening Geoff looked at the writing box – the one his mother had said he must cherish and which could change his life. But he knew so little about it. *Perhaps these antiques experts can tell me something – explain its history and why Mum said it was valuable. Sarah said it was free and one could just turn up.*

And so on Sunday, there he was walking towards Table 20 with the old writing box. He certainly had not expected Ken Parson's reaction.

"Wow – a Henri Tabuteau – I've waited years to see one of these. How exciting."

Geoff was nonplussed, "Are you saying there's something special about this old box?"

"Special? Oh yes – Henri Tabuteau was one of the most skilled cabinet makers of his time. See here on the corners – the shape of the brass fitting is pure Tabuteau and if you look closely – here use my magnifying glass – you can see his monogram of the joined H and T. I'm just so thrilled to see one in the flesh. Thanks for bringing it along. Have you got the key so we can open it up?"

"Yes. But unfortunately I only have the key for the main box – I've never had or even seen the key you need to open the upper compartment."

Geoff was somewhat put out when Ken burst out laughing and clapped his hands together. "Mr Kirkwood, can I call you Geoff? You have fallen into the famous Tabuteau trap – there is only one key."

"But the key I have doesn't open that part. I have tried it many times and it just will not turn – perhaps the lock's broken?"

"So you have no idea what may be hiding in the upper chamber?"

"No – I've never seen it open."

"Mmmm – shall we go exploring? Let me explain. Henri Tabuteau invented a special cabinet lock. You need to put the

161

key in – then pull it out slightly until it can turn – and then you need to turn it around three full turns. Not one, not two but three times. Do you want to or shall I?"

Geoff realized this box needed specialist handling and care so he refrained from taking over. "Go ahead please."

With the key in the upper lock, Ken pulled it back slightly and turned it three full turns. "Ok Geoff – your box – you open it."

With slight trepidation, Geoff lifted the lid and there inside was an envelope. An envelope he had never seen but which bore his name, Geoff Kirkwood, written in his mother's hand writing. Geoff's mind was doing somersaults. *Was this why Mum had insisted I look after the box? Do I open it now in front of all these people? What will it say? Oh Help!*

With trembling hands he opened the envelope and out fell a note and a birth certificate. The note was short and Geoff read it silently to himself.

Dearest Geoff

Please forgive me for not telling you when I was alive but I did not want you to think you were a second best. When I was 15 I had a child but when my parents died in a car crash soon after, I had to give up my darling daughter for adoption. You have a sister somewhere – her name is Marie as you can see on her birth certificate. If you ever find her, tell her I never stopped thinking of her. With all my love – Mum.

Ken waited quietly while Geoff read the note. "I assume from your reaction the note contains a bit of a surprise. If it's too personal, that's fine. It's a lovely box but perhaps under the circumstances we should stop now? What do you say?"

Geoff was almost too stunned to reply. He just looked up at Ken and thanked him for his help and understanding. He then closed the writing box, locked it slowly, picked it up with care and wandered in a daze back to his car.

At home he read and re-read the letter and studied the birth certificate. I have a sister? A sister called Marie and Mum's dog is called Marie. No wonder Mum called the dog Marie. She was right – these two items are certainly changing my life.

He studied the birth certificate in detail. This sister was born locally five years before him. Could she still be alive? Could she still be in this town? How could he begin to find out?

In the office on Monday, Sarah apologized. "Sorry I didn't get to the Fair – did you go? How'd you get on?"

Could he tell her? Why not – it was after all at Sarah's suggestion that he had gone there. So he explained about the box and how Mr Parson had shown him how to open it and how there was a letter inside and before he could stop himself, he had told her all about the contents and the birth certificate.

"Apparently, she was born here in Trentville, 25 October 1975. No more information except that she was called Marie. I almost wish I didn't know – how on earth do I go about finding this person – if she's still here anyway?"

"Did you say 25 October 1975?"

"Yes – that's what's on the birth certificate."

"And she's called Marie?"

"That's the name on the certificate. Why do you ask?"

"Bring the certificate in – we'll look at it tomorrow."

The following day, Sarah was sitting on his desk waiting for him. "Where exactly was this sister born?"

Geoff fished the certificate out of his brief case, "St Andrews Maternity Hospital, here in Trentville."

"What was your mother's name before she was married."

"Karen Thompson."

"No, no – her full name as it appears on the certificate."

"Karen Spencer Thompson – why?"

Sarah took a deep breath, looked straight into Geoff's eyes and made the whole of his world even more topsy turvy.

"I don't quite know how to say this – but it looks like my mother is your sister. The date, the place and the mother's name all match and she's called Marie. Also, Mum told me last night that she was adopted as a baby. I guess that makes you – my uncle."

Sarah could not restrain herself and jumped up throwing her arms around him and giving Uncle Geoff a big hug. She then grabbed the phone and dialled home to tell her mother the news. She was much more excited than Geoff but then Geoff was now in a semi-catatonic state.

"Mum says, would you like to come around on Sunday for lunch? She and Dad would love to meet you – the brother Mum didn't know she had. She also says are you ok with dogs cause they've got a dog in the house? … I'll be there myself, so OK? Yeh? … Twelve o'clock?"

Without fully understanding, Geoff agreed.

Even though it was still early morning, he took the rest of the day off. He needed time on his own to fully understand what had just happened. He now had another Marie in his life. There was Marie the dog, blonde haired Marie on the beach and now a sister he never knew he had, called Marie – who also had – a – dog. Sparkles went off in Geoff's brain. *Oh no. ... This cannot be. Is Marie on the beach and Marie my sister the same person? She's about the right age. That's why we got along so well. ... Thank heavens I never invited her out.*

He tried not to imagine the embarrassment they would both have felt if he had been dating his sister. Ah but relief – *Sarah mentioned her Dad. That means sister Marie, who now is possibly the same person as beach Marie, is married and would not have accepted my invitation anyway. Phew. But we can certainly have a good laugh about it on Sunday.* He even began looking forward to this lunch.

With his heart in his mouth, he rang the door bell at noon on Sunday. Fortunately, Sarah answered and invited him in.

"Mum! Geoff's here – come and meet your brother."

Marie appeared with outstretched hands but Geoff's response was not what was expected. He turned to Sarah, "This is your mother – my sister?"

"Yes," came the hesitant reply.

"But she has brown hair – not blonde."

"Is that a problem?"

"No, no – I – I must have mixed things up. … It's a long story and I'll tell you sometime."

With rekindled interest in this yet a third Marie in his life, he turned and smiled at his newly found sister. "Oh yes – looking at you Marie, I can see you definitely have Mum's eyes and her smile. Come here."

They hugged each other as if they had been close for years. In his mind, Geoff could not quite tell if he was pleased or disappointed that sister Marie was not beach Marie. Sometime he would tell them but not now. Now was the time for getting acquainted with sister Marie and her husband Paul – or should he say brother-in-law.

Having Sarah there made the whole meal much easier and soon everyone was relaxed. Geoff kept answering questions and showing them pictures from an album he had brought along. Even Fiddle, the dog, snuzzled up against Geoff's leg.

At about two thirty the door bell rang. Marie did not seem surprised and she leant over and confided to Geoff. "That'll be Paul's younger sister. She and her ex, Brian, sometimes came on Saturday to take Fiddle out for a walk, but now that Brian's gone, (good riddance), she's made it a regular call on Sunday. She has a dog of her own but her dog and Fiddle get along so well she takes them both out on Sundays. But between you and me, I think she really just wants to see what kind of man is my new found brother. I just can't get over this – I have a younger brother." And she gave him a friendly dig in the arm.

At that point Paul came into the room with his sister.

"Anne-Marie – this is Geoff, Marie's brother."

Geoff and Anne-Marie stared at each other with wide eyes and open mouthed surprise. Anne-Marie was the first to change her expression and broke into the most engaging smile Geoff had ever seen. With a sparkle in her eyes and a quick flick of her blonde hair she spoke with that voice he knew so well.

"You called – I'm here – so do I get any biscuits?"

"Biscuits? Nah – sorry – no biscuits today – but instead, could I suggest dinner for two?"

Geoff racked his brain – *where did that line come from*? The other half of his brain was saying *Thanks Mum, you were right about changing my life!*

As Anne-Marie nodded acceptance of Geoff's invitation, Paul looked from one to the other. "Do you two know each other?"

Anne-Marie chuckled. "In a sort of *'barking'* way I suppose we do – it's a long story – but I think – and I hope – the story's about to get a lot longer."

Printed in Great Britain
by Amazon

87429607R00098